The Hollow Tree

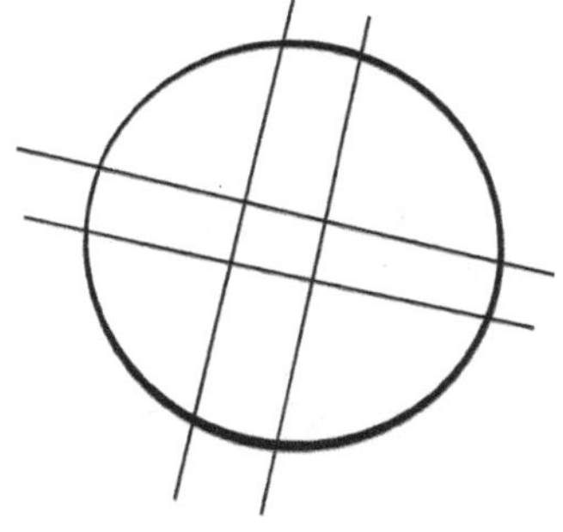

Also by Scott E Adams

The Tales of Blowville

The Hollow Tree
The Cellar Below
The Long Return

The Charlie Randall Chronicles

A Name Stolen

The Hollow Tree

Tales of Blowville

Volume 1

Scott E Adams

Published by:
Scott Adams

ISBN 978-0-9964396-6-4

Table of Contents

Table of Contents (continued)

Foreword

Nestled in the rugged hills of Potter County, Pennsylvania, the town of Blowville once stood as a fleeting but fervent outpost of the timber boom that swept through northern Pennsylvania in the late 19th century. Established along Bailey Run during the height of the hemlock harvest, Blowville was one of many company towns born of the lumber industry's relentless push into the region's untouched forests. With its rough-cut boardwalks, smoke-choked mill yards, and tar-paper shanties, Blowville sprang up nearly overnight, built to serve the needs of a single purpose: extracting the towering hemlocks and tanning bark from the surrounding wilderness.

By the early 1900s, as the hillsides were stripped bare and the economic engine that sustained it ground to a halt, Blowville faded just as quickly as it had risen. Today, little remains of the town beyond a collection of seasonal hunting camps, tucked quietly into the woods where workers once labored and children played. Nature, as always, reclaimed what industry abandoned.

This book is a work of historical fiction. While inspired by real events and locations, and informed by the rhythms of old newspaper clippings, oral histories, and fragmentary records from the time, the people who walk through these pages are imagined. Some are stitched from the brief mention in a forgotten headline. Others are wholly invented. Where actual historical incidents are referenced, they have been adapted to fit the narrative and should not be taken as literal truth.

Any resemblance to real individuals, living or deceased, is purely coincidental and unintended.

The Hollow Tree and the *Tales of Blowville* are, above all, a story. A story of labor and land, of ambition and grief. A story about what remains, after the saws have stopped, after the trees are gone, and after the names fade from memory.

Prologue

October, Present Day — Potter County, Pennsylvania

The forest had long since taken back most of Blowville, but not all of it.

Each year, as the leaves turned and frost crept into the valleys, the old hunting camps along Bailey Run came back to life. Trucks rumbled up the pot-holed road. Smoke curled from chimneys. Men and women returned with rifles, fishing rods, and coolers full of beer. Stories were told around firepits, some true, most not. The same families came back year after year, generations bound not by blood, but by this place.

Among the camps, one stood apart: King's Camp.

Once the sheriff's house, the old two-story structure sat on a gentle rise just above the run. Time had weathered its bones, but it stood firm, roof patched with tin, shutters replaced with mismatched boards, porch reinforced with treated lumber. Inside were bunk beds, a woodstove, old rifles mounted on the wall, and names carved into the doorframe going back sixty years. It was more than just a camp. It was a gathering place.

Marin Clarke knew all this. Her uncle had hunted these woods. Her grandfather too. She'd heard the stories growing up: about snow so deep it buried trucks, about brook trout longer than your forearm, about things seen, or imagined, in the dark timber.

What she hadn't heard until recently was the name: Blowville.

It appeared in a line in an old newspaper article, buried in the archives of the Potter Enterprise: *"...found dead near Blowville... third death since Labor Day."* The year was 1895. And that, to Marin, was a thread worth pulling.

She stood now at the edge of King's Camp, the door creaking behind her. She had come alone, before deer season, with permission from the Kings. The hunters wouldn't be back for weeks. The woods were still, except for the hush of Bailey Run and the occasional flick of a trout's tail.

Inside, the camp smelled of old wood, smoke, and cedar. She swept aside a pile of stacked gear in the back room, a corner no one seemed to use anymore, and noticed a loose board in the wall.

Behind it: a small, iron-hinged box. Blackened by fire. Cool to the touch.

She pried it open.

Inside were fragments of a journal. Fragile pages. Neat, slanted handwriting in faded ink. The first line read:

"This place was never meant to last. Not the trees, not the men, not even the bones. But some things hold on. Some things, even after the fires, refuse to be buried."

— *C. M., Blowville, November 12, 1895*

She turned another page. Then another. A map fragment. Names she didn't recognize. Accusations. Cryptic markings. And circled in pencil: *"The Freck warrant—don't trust Terrence Fee."*

Marin looked up.

Bailey Run whispered outside, just as it always had. But now, beneath the hum of the water, she heard something else.

Blowville was still here. Not alive, exactly.

But not dead either.

Part One

Chapter 1 – Arrival

Late Autumn, 1895 — Blowville, Pennsylvania

The road into Blowville was barely a road at all.

More a scar cut into the hillside, churned to mud by ox teams and logging wagons. Ruts deep enough to swallow a boot angled across the slope, and every curve threatened to slide the cart into the brambles below. The trees leaned in close here, hemlock, mostly. Dark and tall. Silent in a way that made Jonas Webber's shoulders rise, unbidden, as if expecting the snap of a twig behind him.

He flicked the reins gently. The mare responded with a weary grunt.

He'd been on the road three days out of Coudersport. Longer if you counted the time spent waiting for supplies to be loaded at the railhead. His contract was folded in his coat pocket, brittle with creases. *Timber Scaler – Goodyear Brothers Logging, Blowville.* Fourteen dollars a week and a place to sleep.

It would do.

Blowville appeared gradually, as if reluctant to show itself. First the scent, bark and pitch, smoke and tannin. Then sound: a rhythmic pounding like some distant heart, which he would come to learn was the bark mill's pulley hammer. And then the town itself: a row of low, leaning buildings scattered along the banks of Bailey Run, tethered to one another by mud, gossip, and the scent of sap.

He passed a general store with a sagging porch, a cookhouse with wash hung between trees, a half-constructed boarding house, and at last the camp office. A black dog barked once, then thought better of it.

Jonas tied the mare and stepped down stiffly. The cold had set into his joints during the last few miles. He removed his hat, dusted it against his thigh, and knocked.

The man who answered was thick through the chest and wore suspenders over a wool shirt dark with sweat. His sleeves were rolled high enough to show a tattoo on one forearm: a coiled snake with a saber through its eye.

"Webber?" the man asked.

"Jonas Webber."

"Thought you'd be older." He stepped aside. "I'm Anders. Camp boss. Come in."

Inside was warmer. The office smelled of pipe smoke, damp wool, and ink. A stove crackled in the corner. Stacks of timber slips were piled high on the table. Anders handed him a tin cup of coffee; black, bitter, welcome.

"Been a scaler long?" Anders asked.

"Three years," Jonas said. "Allegheny line. Before that, west of Cherry Springs."

Anders grunted. "You'll want to keep close to the bark teams for now. Hemlock's thick on the Freck warrants. That's where we're working next."

Jonas nodded, eyes flicking briefly to a map pinned on the wall. Tracts marked in red crisscrossed the hills above the run. He noted the names, Freck, Fee, Goodyear, and the darker ink strokes where rivers and ravines slashed across the ridges.

"We lost two men last month," Anders said, too casually. "One fell. One drank himself into the creek. Be smart and stay dry."

Jonas said nothing. He hadn't come to make friends.

Anders stared at him a beat too long. Then nodded toward the back. "You're bunked with the others in the scaler's cabin. Supper's at six. If you need a girl or a bottle, you'll find them upstream. Ask for the pig's ear."

Jonas gave a half-smile. “I didn’t come here for either.”

Anders shrugged. “That’ll change.”

Outside, the sky had turned the color of hammered lead. Smoke coiled from chimneys. Men in wool coats moved through the slush, axes slung over shoulders, dogs trailing at their heels. Somewhere downstream, a whistle blew. Jonas turned toward the scaler’s cabin, the journaled hills rising behind him.

Blowville wasn’t much. But for now, it would be home.

* * *

The scaler’s cabin sat a few paces up the slope from the rest of the town, nestled among a stand of wind-bitten spruce. It leaned slightly, like it had grown tired of holding itself upright over the years, but it was solid enough. Jonas opened the door and was met with a wave of heat and the sour musk of damp boots and pipe smoke.

Three men sat around a scarred table, one of them carving a wedge of wood, the other two working through a deck of cards that looked older than the war. They glanced up when Jonas entered.

“You’re the new one,” said the man with the knife, not unkindly.

Jonas nodded. “Webber.”

“Crane.” The man stood and offered his hand, big and rough with bark still clinging under the nails. “And that’s Parks and Holloway. Don’t lend Holloway anything you want back in one piece.”

“You’ll get it back,” Holloway grumbled, “just not in the same condition.”

They chuckled lightly and made space at the table. Jonas set down his pack, pulled off his coat, and accepted a dented tin mug that someone filled with something warm and vaguely alcoholic.

“Where you from?” Crane asked.

“Originally? Juniata County. Been around since.” Jonas sipped. “You all work the Freck?”

“All but Holloway. He’s got a lame wrist, scaling paperwork until it heals,” Crane said, pointing with his thumb. “Freck’s steep country. You’ll earn your pay.”

Jonas nodded slowly. “I’ve worked worse.”

Outside, the wind picked up, rattling the shutters. Someone slammed a door in the distance. The whistle blew again, two short bursts this time. Supper call.

The four of them filed out into the dusk, boots sinking into half-frozen slush. Smoke from the cookhouse chimney caught the last red streaks of daylight, curling upward like the fingers of a tired ghost. Men were already lining up with tin plates and metal cups, voices low, the day’s labor hanging heavy on their shoulders.

The cook, an enormous, silent man named Hagarty, slopped stew into bowls with practiced indifference. Jonas found a seat on a bench near the end and ate slowly, watching the room.

There were easily fifty men packed in; loggers, bark peelers, mule handlers, sawyers. A few glanced his way. None said much. He didn’t mind.

“First night’s the quiet one,” Crane said, sliding in beside him. “Tomorrow, the noise starts.”

“What kind of noise?” Jonas asked.

Crane shrugged. “Depends how much rain we get. Mud brings trouble. Always does.”

As the meal wound down, a tall man in a black coat and battered bowler entered. His presence drew a few nods but no words. He carried himself with the assurance of someone who belonged everywhere and nowhere all at once. Jonas watched him.

“That’s Fee,” Crane muttered. “Terrence Fee. Owns half the warrants we’re cutting. And probably the other half too, through some paper or another. Don’t cross him.”

Jonas didn’t answer. But something in his gut stirred, a slow and familiar unease.

Later, after the plates were scraped clean and men had drifted toward their bunks or toward town for drink and smoke, Jonas walked alone to the edge of camp. Bailey Run murmured through the dark below, a constant thread of sound winding between the trees. He stood there, hands in pockets, eyes fixed on the line where the forest met the sky.

There was something about this place. Something in the way the trees stood so close together. In the silence that waited after each gust of wind. In the black water curling through the brush.

He took a long breath, turned, and went back to his bunk.

Chapter 2 – Clara's Ledger

Late Autumn, 1895 — Blowville

Clara Moran never intended to keep a ledger of the town. But once she started, she couldn't stop.

It began with small notes, who visited the store, who arrived by wagon, who left without saying goodbye. She wrote them in the back pages of her father's almanac, behind weather predictions and tide charts that didn't matter much in the hills. At first, it was just something to do. A way to mark time in a town where time moved like tree sap, slow, but always down.

Now she kept a dedicated book. Leather-bound. Hidden beneath the floorboard beneath her bed, just to the right of a knothole she could find with her toe in the dark.

She inked the morning's entry carefully:

October 29, 1895 – Another new man arrived today. Alone. Looks like a soldier, though he wears no badge or medal. He watched everyone at supper like he was memorizing them. I'll wager five cents he carries more than a measuring stick.

She paused, tapping the nib of her pen against her chin. Then added:

His name is Jonas Webber. I will watch him, as I do the others.

From outside the window came the faint crack of an axe, then the creak of a cart axle. She stood and moved toward the sill. The Moran house overlooked much of the town, a carpenter's perch, her father called it. Built sturdily and early, before Goodyear's crews had poured into the hollow and turned the run into a logging chute.

Down below, Jonas was walking the path between the scaler's cabin and the edge of the clearing. He moved like a man used to silence. Watchful. Careful with his weight.

Clara narrowed her eyes.

She'd grown up with men like him. They passed through Blowville often. Some stayed a season, some a week. Most were hard with work and harder with drink. A few left behind children. One or two left behind graves.

But Webber didn't seem like most.

Behind her, her father's saw rasped through lumber. William Harvey Moran was building a set of new bunks for the boarding house. The Fee Brothers had promised him good coin for it. Business was strong now. Everyone said so.

Clara had heard that before.

She set down her journal, wiped her hands, and pulled her shawl around her shoulders.

"Where are you off to?" her father asked as she reached the door.

"Library," she said, without looking back.

William chuckled. "Girl, you are the library."

It wasn't untrue. The schoolhouse only had a handful of books, most tattered, and she had read them all twice. But the shelves also held old land maps, correspondence from the Goodyear office, and teacher's logs from years when the town had nearly gone silent.

Clara wasn't interested in fairy tales. She was searching for patterns.

She crossed town quietly, nodding to the bark haulers and mule boys. The air smelled of sap and leather, with a bitter undertone she recognized as tannin from the mill vats. At the corner near the saloon, commonly called pig's ears in these parts, a group of woodsmen were already drunk. One tipped his cap to her; she did not return the gesture.

In the schoolhouse, she lit a lamp and opened a folder marked *Misc. – 1888–89*. Inside were clippings, receipts, and one folded surveyor's sketch. She spread it across the table.

The same symbols again. Carved into the corners like decoration, or maybe something else. She traced them with her fingertip. Four intersecting lines over a hollowed circle.

They matched the one she had found scratched into the back of her own ledger.

Someone had drawn it before her.

Someone who had watched this place like she did.

She leaned closer, the flame flickering across her page, and whispered aloud:

"What are you trying to tell me?"

Behind her, the wind picked up.

And far off, down Bailey Run, something made the dogs bark.

* * *

The dogs were still barking when Clara stepped outside the schoolhouse, their chorus echoing from somewhere near the trestle bridge down by the run. It could've been a coyote. Or a bear. Or just the wind rolling off the ridge tops in a way the animals didn't like.

The truth was, things always sounded different in Blowville after dark. The logging camps slowed but never stopped. Men wandered from campfires to shanties, from card tables to fights, from the pig's ear to the ditch. And the woods, especially the hemlocks, always whispered something when the sun went down. Even the bark mill, which shut its belts at dusk, seemed to hum with leftover noise.

She pulled her shawl tighter.

From where she stood, she could see most of the town. It had grown fast, faster than it should've. A cookhouse, blacksmith, and general store anchored the lower end of Main Street, where the oxen teams clattered through by day and the drunks staggered past by night. The boarding house sat across from the scaler's cabin, with a new bunkhouse rising behind it. Her father had built most of them. William Harvey Moran's work framed Blowville in wood and nail.

Past that, the land gave way to the muddy edge of Bailey Run. It curved like a lazy snake through the hollow, swollen from the recent rains. On its banks stood the bark mill, three stories of timber and tin, its vats reeking of tannin and steam, and beyond it, the drying yard where strips of peeled hemlock bark were stacked like cordwood to dry.

Upstream, thin plumes of smoke marked the sites of smaller logging camps. She knew the names by heart: Crow Hollow, Fee's Claim, Number Four. Men came down from them on Saturdays for supplies and sin, and sometimes never went back.

Farther still, the woods thickened, rising into the Freck warrant, a tract everyone talked about and few dared to walk after dusk.

She made her way back home just as the lanterns in the boarding house flickered on, casting yellow light into the cold, early dark. The mud sucked at her boots. The porch boards creaked as she stepped inside the Moran house. Her father looked up from his plans at the table, a pencil tucked behind his ear.

"You find what you were looking for?" he asked.

"I found part of something."

He smiled faintly. "Well, you always do."

Clara wanted to ask him if he remembered anything about the survey symbols she'd seen. But he looked tired. He always looked tired these days. The jobs were steady, but the pace was punishing. Even a good carpenter needed time to rest, and there was precious little of that in a town like Blowville.

Outside, voices rose near the pig's ear. A shout, a splash, laughter that didn't quite sound joyful.

Blowville was growing. It was a company town, sure, but it had a pulse all its own. Too fast, sometimes. Too hungry. And Clara had begun to wonder if the town was shaping the men who lived in it, or if they were reshaping the town into something darker.

She moved to the window, her reflection barely visible in the glass.

A lantern swung on a post outside the cookhouse. A man's silhouette passed beneath it, tall, solitary. Jonas Webber again. Heading somewhere with purpose, or maybe with ghosts.

She didn't know which yet.

But she would.

And she would write it all down.

Chapter 3 – The Freck Warrant

November 1, 1895 — Blowville

Jonas woke before the whistle.

The air in the scaler's cabin was cold enough to see his breath. He dressed quickly; wool shirt, suspenders, oilskin coat. The others still slept, curled beneath quilts that stank of sweat and cedar shavings. Outside, the sky was bruised purple. Bailey Run muttered just beyond the trees.

He liked mornings like this. Cold. Quiet. Before the saws started screaming and the camp came alive with shouting and steam.

By the time the ox teams were loaded, he was already walking ahead, boots crunching frost, journal and rule stick in his pack. The crew's destination was the northeast section of the Freck warrant, a thick stretch of timber that had resisted previous crews. Too steep. Too dark. But Goodyear Brothers wanted every last bark-worthy hemlock brought down before spring.

Three mules passed him on the trail, their handlers half-awake, chewing plug tobacco and swearing about the slope. Jonas gave a short nod but didn't stop.

The Freck tract loomed above the run like a cathedral. The hemlocks here were old, three feet thick at the base, their limbs blocking the light even at midday. Moss covered everything. Bark hung in heavy curls. Fog clung to the ground.

Jonas paused and set down his pack. The first job was scaling, a rough estimation of what was worth cutting, what could be peeled for bark, and what was too twisted or rotten to bother with. He unrolled the ledger, marked the section number, and walked to the first tree.

He placed a hand on the trunk. The bark was rough, dense with age.

34-inch diameter.
Sound bark. Straight run.
Grade: Prime.

He wrote it down.

The work settled him. Numbers. Angles. Tangible things. He moved from tree to tree, marking trunks with chalk and cataloging estimates. But as the sun climbed, what little of it pierced the hemlock canopy, he noticed something strange.

Every few trees, a carving.

Small. Faint. Always at eye level.

Not lumberman marks, not symbols for directional fall, slope danger, or rot. These were different. Simple designs: intersecting lines, circles, occasionally a figure that looked almost like a branch with five notches.

Jonas rubbed one with his thumb. It had been cut long ago, years, maybe decades. Older than this season's crew.

He didn't mark it in the official log. But in the back of his own notebook, he drew one of the symbols. Just in case.

"Webber!" a voice called up from the slope.

It was Crane, slogging uphill, sweat already darkening his collar. "You planning on counting the moss too? We're ready to drop that run!"

Jonas gave a tight nod and tucked the notebook away.

By midday, four trees had been felled. The noise echoed down the hollow like cannon fire. Mule teams strained against harnesses. Bark peelers followed behind, stripping the thick brown slabs off the trunks with sharp spuds, piling them in cribs to dry.

Jonas worked in rhythm. Record, mark, move.

And yet, always that itch between his shoulders. A sense of being watched.

Once, while he was bent over a stump taking a measure, he caught sight of movement in the woods. Not a man. Not an animal. Just... absence. A shift in the trees. A pause in the sound of wind.

When he looked again, there was nothing.

At sundown, the work ceased. Men lit pipes and drank coffee near the tool wagon. Jonas sat apart, notebook in hand, recording the day's counts by fading light. Crane sat beside him, wordless for a time.

"You feel it too, don't you?" Crane said finally.

Jonas didn't look up. "Feel what?"

"This tract," Crane muttered. "Don't smell right. Don't sound right. And those carvings?"

Jonas glanced at him now. "You've seen them."

Crane nodded. "They're older than us. Some say the Indians marked trees like that. Others say the first loggers did it to warn off the next crew."

"Warn them of what?"

Crane stared into the fire. "Depends who you ask."

A long silence passed.

Then Jonas said, quietly, "Anyone ever go missing up here?"

Crane didn't answer for a while.

Then: "Seven winters ago. A peeler named Maddox. Just vanished. No tracks. Just gone."

Jonas didn't reply. He folded his notebook, rose, and began the walk back to camp.

Behind him, the trees swayed without wind.

And somewhere deep in the Freck, a low creaking echoed, like wood under strain.

* * *

The path down from the Freck was narrower than he remembered.

Jonas moved carefully in the fading light, his boots crunching through frost-rimmed leaves, the sounds of the crew already fading behind him. The others would stay a bit longer, share their drink, curse the trees, maybe gamble under lantern light. He preferred the quiet.

But quiet wasn't what he found.

The deeper he walked, the louder the forest seemed. Not with the rustle of animals or the whisper of the run, but with something else. A layered hum, like the memory of sound. The kind you hear just before thunder.

He shook it off.

The slope steepened, and he adjusted his footing, grabbing a branch to steady himself, then stopped. His hand had landed on a notched limb, smoothed by age and worn in the center. Another symbol had been carved here, half-concealed beneath lichen. Not just a slash mark. Something intentional.

He pulled out his notebook, traced it as best he could by what light remained. A circle, closed tight, and within it, a tree split down the center.

He didn't know why it unsettled him. Just that it did.

The hair on his arms rose.

He heard the stream before he saw it, Bailey Run, winding below, its water black in the dusk. And then he saw it: the edge of a clearing, strange in shape, roughly oval. No stumps. No signs of recent cutting. Just open ground beneath the trees.

The clearing hadn't been marked on the crew's map.

Jonas stepped into it.

The forest sound dropped. Not disappeared, dropped, like someone had turned down the volume on the world. Even Bailey Run felt quieter here, despite being only a few paces away.

At the center of the space stood a single, dead hemlock, split down the middle, its core black and hollowed, as if struck by lightning long ago.

He circled it slowly.

At the base were more carvings. Symbols like the ones he'd seen earlier, but tighter together. Some had been gouged over each other, layers of warning, or record.

And at the base, just beneath a curled root, he spotted something else.

A metal tag, nailed into the bark. Old. Nearly rusted through.

He crouched.

There were letters. Barely legible in the dying light:

MADDOX 1887

Jonas stood slowly, every hair on his neck stiff with cold.

He turned back toward camp.

Didn't run. Didn't hurry.

But the way the shadows moved behind him, the way the trees seemed to lean just slightly inward, it felt like the woods had taken note of him.

That night, back in the scaler's cabin, he said nothing.

He ate. He lay in his bunk. He listened to the wind.

But long after the others were snoring, Jonas sat up, pulled out his notebook, and wrote a single line in the back cover:

The woods remember things. And they mark the men who forget that.

Chapter 4 – Paper and Ash

November 2, 1895 — Blowville

Clara woke to the smell of smoke and pine tar.

It drifted in through the cracked window above her bed, mingling with the scent of paper and ink that had come to define her room. She had fallen asleep over her ledger again, the spine pressing a red crease into her cheek. When she sat up, the journal's pages crackled like dry leaves.

She scanned the last few entries, shorthand notes on crew movements, wagon deliveries, changes in bark pricing, but her eyes lingered on the one from the night before:

"The symbol again, on the survey map and carved into the teacher's desk leg. A circle with four lines, crossed in the center. It matches the one in the old ledger I found in the Fee file drawer. What does it mean?"

She had asked herself that question a dozen times in as many ways. No one else in Blowville seemed to notice. Or they noticed, and pretended not to.

Downstairs, her father was prepping his tools, getting ready to head to his shop to carve beams for a bunkhouse that would house the next wave of seasonal workers. William Harvey Moran rose with the sun and rarely stopped until it disappeared again.

Clara dressed, tied her hair, and wrapped herself in her heavy wool shawl. The morning was bitter, sky pale and low, the scent of snow lurking behind the frost.

On her way to the schoolhouse, she passed two bark wagons loaded with raw hemlock strips. The oxen steamed in the cold. One of the drivers tipped his cap and called out, "Winter's comin', Miss Moran."

"It always does," she replied.

Inside the schoolhouse, she lit the stove, pulled on gloves with the fingers cut out, and spread the latest map copy across the teacher's desk. This one was newer, dated 1889, but still carried traces of older hands. The same tracts. The same streambeds. And tucked into the northern quadrant near the Freck warrant: a faint oval drawn in pencil, circled, but unlabeled.

She ran her finger over it.

A hollow? A clearing?

She had only seen it referenced once before, in the old tannery account logs. A vague note beside a lost bark load: *"Load never made it past the open."*

The open. Was that what they called it?

Clara sat down, pulled the coded pages of her journal closer, and turned to a fresh sheet. But before she could begin writing, a voice startled her.

"You always keep your head buried in old ink, or just most days?"

She turned sharply.

Jonas Webber stood just inside the doorway. His coat was dusted with frost. His boots were clean, but his eyes weren't, dark under the brow, like someone who hadn't slept.

"I didn't hear you knock," Clara said, more coolly than she meant to.

"I didn't," he replied, stepping further in. "Didn't mean to interrupt. Just thought someone ought to know... there's a tree up past the Freck that's got Maddox's name on it."

She stood up now, her heart ticking faster.

"Maddox? The peeler who disappeared?"

Jonas nodded. “A rusted name tag. Nailed to a split trunk. Can’t be recent. Ground was untouched. Carvings too, older than your maps.”

She stepped closer, hesitant. “Why are you telling me this?”

“Because I’ve seen you watching. Taking notes. Looking at the town the same way I do.”

There was no accusation in his tone, just fact.

She studied him for a long moment. Then reached beneath the desk, pulled out a sheaf of copied maps, and laid them flat between them.

“I think someone marked that area off the books,” she said quietly. “The oval shows up once. No labels. But it’s always just north of the Freck, tucked between tributaries. Like a missing piece of the puzzle.”

Jonas nodded. “I found it. Last night. It doesn’t feel right.”

She looked at him then, not just glanced, but looked, and saw in his face the same unease she’d felt in the bones of the town for months. Something shifting. Something waking.

“We need to go back,” she said.

He raised an eyebrow. “We?”

Clara’s voice was steady.

“If you want to understand what’s out there, you’ll need more than numbers and trees. You’ll need someone who’s been watching longer.”

He didn’t smile. But he didn’t argue either.

Outside, snow began to fall, light at first, like a whisper from the hills.

And down along Bailey Run, the wind carried the scent of bark, ash, and something older still.

* * *

They left town just after noon.

Clara wore a gray cloak lined in flannel, too fine for the woods but thick enough to keep the wind out. Jonas offered her a second set of oilskin gaiters from the scaler's cabin; she accepted them without comment.

The trail was quieter than usual. Most of the crew had shifted down-valley to work easier terrain before the weather turned worse. The higher tracts were all but abandoned now, save for a few teams wrapping up the bark haul.

Snow fell steadily as they climbed, dusting the hemlocks and blurring the path behind them. Bailey Run moved below, muffled under white. Clara kept pace beside Jonas, matching his stride without difficulty. She had the bearing of someone who'd grown up walking ridge lines and muddy inclines.

"You've done this before," he said, not turning.

She nodded. "My grandpa was a scaler. Took me with him at times, before he moved back home to the farm. We walked all over this valley."

"You believe Maddox is up here?" he asked.

"I believe something is. Something worth hiding."

Jonas said nothing.

They reached the edge of the Freck warrant by early afternoon. The air changed the moment they stepped beneath the canopy. The wind disappeared. The trees grew too close together. Their breath steamed in the cold, but no sound rose above the hush of snowfall on needles.

Clara stopped beside the first marked tree. Her gloved fingers traced the carved lines. "These aren't timber codes."

"I know."

"Some of them resemble old Iroquois land signs," she added. "Warning symbols. Boundaries."

He looked at her. "You studied that?"

"Not formally," she said. "But long enough to know when something was meant to be seen, and when it was meant to be felt."

They pressed deeper. The clearing came into view slowly, like a memory returning. That same unnatural oval of space, no stumps, no saplings, just open forest floor, dusted with snow. And at its center, the split hemlock, skeletal against the white.

Clara stepped toward it, the dead branches above her creaking like ancient bones.

"This place isn't natural," she whispered.

Jonas pointed toward the trunk. The metal tag still clung to the bark, half-swallowed by years of growth.

MADDOX 1887

She crouched low, brushing away snow near the roots. "There's more," she said. "Fresh." She pulled a twig aside to reveal boot prints, partially frozen but clear. "Someone's been here within the past week."

"Crew?"

"No one's supposed to be cutting up here this week," she said, standing. "And this path," she pointed to a line of trampled snow heading into the undergrowth, "goes away from the logging roads."

They exchanged a glance.

Then, silently, they followed.

The trail led to a narrow gulley framed by frost-covered ferns and winding deer paths. The air grew colder. The trees leaned in. Jonas unshouldered his measuring stick, not as a tool now, but as something to hold between him and the dark.

Clara stepped carefully over a fallen log, and gasped.

Before them, nestled beneath a crooked pine, was a small pile of stones, like a crude grave. Laid atop it, half-buried in snow, was a man's boot, torn, laces frayed, the leather split at the seam.

Jonas stepped forward and nudged the stones aside with the tip of his boot.

Underneath, something metallic caught the light.

Clara crouched. Brushed away snow and leaves.

A pocketknife. Closed. Bloodstained. And beside it, a tag similar to Maddox's, but the name had been scratched out, violently.

Only the date remained:

1892

She looked up at Jonas.

"We need to tell someone," she said.

Jonas's eyes were still on the scratched-out name. "Tell them what? That we found a rock pile, bad memories, and an old metal tag?"

"We found a grave."

"Or someone wants us to think we did."

A branch snapped somewhere beyond the gully, sharp and close.

They both turned toward the sound, hearts suddenly loud in their chests.

Nothing. Just falling snow.

“Come on,” Jonas said, voice low. “Let’s get back before we become part of the next story.”

Chapter 5 – The Business of Shadows

November 3, 1895 — Blowville

Terrence Fee believed in two things: ownership and silence.

He owned more timberland than any other man in Potter County, though not all of it bore his name. Some titles were wrapped in the skirts of dummy corporations or filed under cousins who couldn't spell "deed." Others were still contested, but that never stopped his men from peeling the bark or dropping the trees. Fee Brothers didn't wait on lawyers.

And as for silence, it was the only thing that kept a place like Blowville running.

He stood at the back window of his office above the mill, watching the steam rise from the vats. His boots were polished, his coat tailored in Buffalo and still stiff at the shoulders. On the desk behind him sat a half-empty glass of rye, sweating into a ring on the ledger paper.

A knock at the door.

He didn't turn. "If it's Crane, tell him the haul slips can wait. If it's the sheriff, I'm not in."

"It's neither," came the voice. Calm. Measured.

Fee turned slowly.

A man stood just inside the door, coat dripping from the snow, hat in hand. Pale eyes. Thin scar across his chin. He hadn't heard the door open.

Fee narrowed his eyes. "You've got two seconds to tell me who sent you."

"No one sent me, Mr. Fee. Just passing word."

"Word about what?"

The man stepped forward, placed a folded piece of paper on the desk, and pushed it across with one gloved finger.

Fee didn't move. "Go on."

The man tilted his head. "Someone's been poking around the Freck. Too far north. Found the open."

Fee's jaw flexed. "Who?"

"New scaler. Webber. And the girl, Moran's daughter."

Clara. He should've known. Always reading, always watching.

He picked up the note. Unfolded it. Ink smudged from snow, but legible:

The name tag is still there. And they've found the second one.

He folded it again, slowly.

"You said they were just looking," Fee said.

"They are," the man replied. "For now."

Silence stretched long and tight.

Then Fee said, almost gently, "Do you know what happens if they ask the wrong questions? If they start talking to the wrong people?"

"I imagine," the man said, "that it gets very quiet again."

Fee looked out the window. The town moved below him, loggers with sacks over shoulders, oxen dragging stripped trunks, boys hauling water. Blowville thrived because it obeyed gravity. Trees fell. Men followed orders. And no one climbed uphill unless they had a reason.

"I want eyes on both of them," Fee said. "Discreet. If they go back into the woods, I want to know exactly where, how far, and if they come back."

The man gave a half-smile. "And if they don't?"

"Then we bury it." Fee took the rye glass and tossed it back. "Like everything else in this damn town."

The man nodded once, turned, and slipped out the door without sound.

Fee sat alone now, watching the bark smoke rise and curl above the town.

In a few more years, the hemlock would be gone. The hills stripped. The company would move on, maybe south, maybe west. The men would scatter. But while it lasted, Blowville would remain his.

And no one, no girl with a journal, no quiet-eyed scaler, not even the dead, was going to take that from him.

Chapter 6 – The Sound of Wood Splitting

November 5, 1895 — Blowville

Elmer Fields had been Blowville's carpenter for eight years, four months, and, as of that morning, seventeen days.

He knew because he kept track the way a man tracks rings in a tree, counting quietly, marking time by jobs completed and boards replaced. His hands had helped raise nearly every structure in the hollow: the cookhouse roof after the spring thaw of '89, the porch rail on the post office, the new joists under the pig's ear when too many drunks got rowdy and collapsed the floor.

Wood talked if you knew how to listen. And lately, it had been groaning under its own weight.

He stood now beside the plank wall of the Moran house, fitting a shutter hinge with care. William Moran was inside, drafting measurements for the next boarding house. Clara had passed him earlier with her head down, cheeks flushed with cold and focus. She barely saw Elmer when she passed anymore, not out of rudeness, but out of purpose.

"Elmer!" a voice called from down the road. It was Dan Mullin, the tanner's apprentice, his face pale beneath his cap. "You heard about Ebenspecker?"

Elmer straightened slowly. "No. What about him?"

"Dead," Mullin said, catching his breath. "Found in the creek. Just past the bend near King's Camp. Gash in the back of his head like he'd been split by an axe."

Elmer said nothing for a long moment.

"That makes three now," he said finally. "Since summer."

Mullin nodded. "Sheriff says he slipped. Too much drink."

"He slipped uphill?" Elmer muttered. "Back of the head's a strange place for a fall."

"People are saying..." Mullin glanced around. "Well. People are saying the Freck's cursed."

Elmer sighed and wiped his hands on a rag. "It's not cursed," he said. "It's just tired of being cut into."

But as the boy walked off, Elmer felt the cold in his joints in a new way. George Ebenspecker hadn't been the brightest, nor the cleanest, but he'd been strong. A woodsman. The kind who knew how to make it home drunk and barefoot if he had to.

And yet now he was the third man in as many months to turn up dead.

Back in his workshop, Elmer turned to his bench. A pine plank sat ready to be shaped into the last brace for the Fee Brothers' new bunkhouse. He set the blade against it, but didn't cut.

Instead, he reached under the bench and pulled out an old box, the hinges rusted, the wood warped. Inside were odds and ends from his early years in Blowville, nails made by hand, a folded sketch of the first scaler's cabin, and a thin packet of papers he hadn't opened in years.

He unfolded them slowly.

Survey maps. Older than the town itself. Lines drawn by men long gone. Symbols in the margins, some that matched the marks Clara had shown him years ago when she was still too young to ask questions out loud.

One circle caught his eye. Near the top of the Freck warrant.

Beneath it, in faded ink, a note in an unfamiliar hand:

"Do not build beyond this line. Water turns. Bark blackens."

Elmer stared at it for a long time. Then folded the papers and tucked them into his coat.

He needed to speak to Clara.

And to Jonas Webber, if he could find him.

Because Blowville was no longer just a town on the banks of Bailey Run. It was a wound. And someone, or something, had begun to pick at the stitches.

* * *

Elmer found them near the edge of town, down where the path curved toward the old mill pond. Clara was seated on a fallen log, sketchbook in her lap, charcoal staining her fingers. Jonas stood nearby with his coat collar turned up, arms crossed, scanning the treeline as if expecting it to move.

They both looked up as Elmer approached, his breath misting in the cold air.

“I was hoping I’d find the two of you together,” he said, voice low but firm.

Clara set her charcoal aside. “Is it about Ebenspecker?”

Elmer nodded. “Dan Mullin came running. Gash in the back of the head. Found him face-down in the run, not a hundred yards from the clearing you walked into.”

Jonas tensed. “That was two days ago.”

“Which means he died after you left,” Elmer said. “And if someone’s trying to send a message, they’re not whispering anymore.”

Clara stood, brushing snow off her skirt. “You’ve seen the symbols, haven’t you?”

Elmer didn’t answer right away. He reached into his coat and pulled out the folded paper, the old survey note, yellowed at the edges, lines drawn by a hand long dead. He opened it slowly and pointed to the circle near the top of the Freck.

"This was drawn before the mill. Before the company even set up shop. I kept it because I liked the linework. But now..."

He let the sentence hang.

Clara stepped closer. "Water turns. Bark blackens," she read aloud. "What does that mean?"

"I don't know," Elmer said. "But I know it's not just folklore. I was here when Maddox disappeared. One minute he was drinking at the pig's ear, next he's gone. I helped search for him. We went up into the Freck, found tracks that just... stopped. Like the woods swallowed him whole."

Jonas looked down at the paper, then back at Elmer. "Why keep it quiet all these years?"

Elmer's jaw clenched. "Because this town only survives if it doesn't look too hard at the shadows. Fee knows that. So does everyone else in charge."

Clara nodded slowly. "Then we're the ones who look."

Elmer gave her a long, searching look, then a short, approving nod. "You've got a fire in you. Just don't burn yourself with it."

He folded the map again, pressing it into Clara's hands. "Keep this. I trust you'll know when to use it."

A gust of wind kicked through the trees. Somewhere down the run, a hound barked once, then fell silent.

Jonas shifted on his feet. "If we're going to do this, we do it soon. Snow's coming heavy by the end of the week."

"And people are watching," Elmer added. "Fee's already sniffing around."

Clara tucked the map into her satchel. "Then we go back. One more time. And we see what the clearing was meant to hide."

None of them spoke for a moment.

Then Elmer said, almost softly, “Be careful. The woods don’t forget. And they don’t always forgive.”

Chapter 7 – The Line Between Order and Quiet

November 6, 1895 — Blowville

Sheriff Horace Farnsworth did not like trouble, and he especially didn't like trouble that whispered.

He preferred things loud and clear; fistfights outside the pig's ear, bootleg stills in the hollow, the occasional dispute over a broken fence or a stolen mule. Things a man could see, settle, and set straight. But trouble like this, the kind that started in the woods and came back with stories, it made his teeth ache.

He stood now on the back porch of the town jail, pipe clenched in his jaw, watching the sleet turn the rutted road to slush. Across the street, a group of bark haulers moved in slow, deliberate silence, eyes cast down. The usual jokes and curses were missing this morning.

The town had shifted. He could feel it in the way the dogs barked longer than usual. In the silence around the fire pits. In the growing absence of laughter.

George Ebenspecker's death wasn't sitting right with him.

He'd seen plenty of drunk men fall. He'd dragged more than a few out of Bailey Run himself. But the wound on Ebenspecker's head had been too clean. Too deliberate. And the body had been found upstream from where the man was last seen drinking.

Which meant one of two things: he'd wandered in a stupor against the current, or someone had dumped him there, hoping the cold water would do the rest.

A bootstep behind him.

Deputy Stevens. Young, smart, and still green enough to think things could be done proper. He handed over a folded note.

"Found this tacked to the back of the schoolhouse," he said. "No signature. Just the word *'Maddox'* and this."

Farnsworth unfolded the paper. A hand-drawn version of the same circle-and-cross symbol he'd seen carved into trees up on the Freck back in '87.

The sheriff exhaled slowly through his nose.

"They're stirring it up," he said.

"Who?"

"Doesn't matter." He folded the paper again. "They're going into the woods. Again. And they're not doing it for logging rights."

"Want me to stop them?"

"No," Farnsworth said after a long pause. "I want you to watch them. Quietly. Don't interfere. Don't spook Fee either."

Stevens frowned. "You really think Fee's involved?"

Farnsworth looked out across the street again. A boy ran past, chasing a chicken. A man tripped in the slush and muttered an oath. A woman haggled over flour at the store.

"Fee's always involved," the sheriff said. "Whether or not he signs his name."

He tapped the ashes from his pipe and slid it back into his coat.

"I've kept this town balanced on the edge of a blade for eight years," he said. "Between the company, the law, and the truth. But if something's coming up from those woods…" His voice trailed off.

Stevens shifted uneasily. "You think they'll find it?"

"I think," Farnsworth said slowly, "they already have."

Chapter 8 – The Hollow Tree

November 7, 1895 — Freck Warrant

They left before dawn.

Clara carried her satchel, packed with her journal, a copy of the old survey map Elmer had given her, a small lantern, and two thick pencils wrapped in cloth. Jonas carried a scaled-down tool kit, hatchet, measuring stick, a coil of waxed cord, and tucked a flask of strong coffee into his coat.

Neither of them spoke much as they followed Bailey Run northward, frost crunching underfoot, the woods brittle with cold. Snow clung to the branches above like parchment ready to tear.

They didn't need to discuss the risk. They both understood it. The last time they'd come here, they'd left with more questions than answers, and a dead man had surfaced in the creek the next day.

They passed the clearing line before the sun crested the eastern ridge.

Immediately, the air changed. Again.

It was subtle, but undeniable, a kind of hush, as if the woods were holding their breath. Even the stream beside them seemed to run quieter, the sound dampened by something more than snow.

The clearing appeared before them like a wound in the forest.

Jonas stopped first. Clara came to his side. Together they looked at the split hemlock, still standing, hollowed and dark.

But something was different this time.

"There's smoke," Clara whispered.

Thin, pale, rising from the ground near the base of the dead tree. Jonas dropped to one knee, gloved fingers brushing back snow and moss.

A small fire pit, still warm. Buried beneath damp bark strips and a pile of stones.

“Someone was here,” Jonas said. “Hours ago. Maybe less.”

He stood and scanned the tree line. Nothing moved. No prints led in or out.

Clara stepped toward the hemlock. Her boots pressed into the snow with careful purpose.

“I think this was a boundary,” she said. “A marker between tracts. Between things older than maps.”

Jonas ran a hand along the tree’s split core. His fingers found grooves, fresh ones, not the old weathered symbols, but new carvings, etched in haste.

He pulled his measuring stick and used the straight edge to sweep snow from the exposed inner trunk.

“What is it?” Clara asked.

Jonas stepped aside.

There, carved into the heartwood, was a word, not a symbol, cut deep:

“BELOW”

Clara’s breath caught.

Jonas tapped the ground near the base of the tree. “There’s a hollow under here. Listen.”

He stomped his heel once. A dull thump answered, empty and wide.

Together, they cleared snow, moss, and bark until they

revealed a rotted plank, set like a trapdoor over the roots. The wood crumbled at Jonas's touch, revealing a dark space beneath the tree. A cold draft rose up from the hole; wet, earthy, metallic.

Jonas lit the lantern and lowered it into the hollow.

Wooden steps, hand-hewn and ancient, descended into blackness. Just beyond the light's edge, the space widened into a rough chamber. Stone. Timber bracing. A structure hidden beneath the roots.

Clara looked at Jonas. "It's a cellar."

"An old one at that," he said. "Looks like this was built before the town, or shortly after."

They exchanged a look. No words passed. They understood.

Jonas tested the first step. It held. He descended slowly, lantern in hand. Clara followed.

The ladder led into a low chamber, no taller than a man, the ceiling braced with hemlock beams blackened by time and smoke. The smell of rot and iron hung thick. Along the far wall sat a row of crates, weathered and sealed with pitch.

Jonas pried one open with his blade.

Inside: papers, wrapped in oilskin, and something else beneath them, heavy and metallic.

He pulled it out.

A badge. Rusted. Bent. Still legible.

PC Constable – 1886

Clara froze.

Her pulse quickened as the lantern's light wavered in her hand.

“My grandfather was constable then,” she said quietly. “Ezekiel Moran.”

Jonas looked up. “You’re sure?”

She nodded slowly, eyes locked on the tarnished metal. “He left when I was seven. Said he was going home to help my aunt on the farm. That’s what my father told me.”

Her fingers traced the faint lettering along the edge of the badge, the worn star pressed into its center. “But this… this shouldn’t be here. He took it with him when he left.”

Jonas turned the badge over. The back was stained dark, the pin twisted and broken. “If it’s his, someone wanted it buried.”

Clara swallowed hard, a tremor in her voice. “Or someone wanted him buried.”

She lifted the lantern higher. On the wall behind the crates, scratched deep into the timber, was the same symbol they’d seen carved into trees and maps, larger now, deliberate. Four lines intersecting over a circle.

Clara reached into her satchel, unfolded the map Elmer had given her, and held it to the wall. The mark aligned perfectly with the clearing.

“It wasn’t just a warning,” she murmured. “It was a seal.”

And someone had broken it.

Jonas’s voice fell to a whisper. “What the hell was down here?”

A cold breath of air rose from the floor, sour, almost metallic.

Then, above them, the wood groaned.

They turned together.

Footsteps.

Heavy. Deliberate. Coming from the clearing above.

Jonas doused the lantern.

Darkness swallowed them whole.

* * *

Above the hollow, snow fell in slow spirals, whispering down through the canopy in a hush that seemed deliberate.

The footsteps stopped just beyond the edge of the stairs, heavy boots, pausing at the edge of the broken plank Jonas and Clara had uncovered.

A long silence followed. Then, a voice:

“Well now... I told them you two were getting too curious.”

It was Crane.

Not Crane the bark scaler. Not the laughing, sharp-eyed man who joked over stew and card games. That version had slipped off like a worn coat. What remained in the clearing now was something quieter. Harder. A man carrying a different kind of weight.

Jonas and Clara crouched in the dark beneath the tree, listening as Crane shifted his stance. Snow packed beneath his boots.

“I followed you once already,” he said. “Didn’t stop you. Thought maybe you’d scare yourselves off. Thought the woods would do what they always do.”

Another step forward.

“But you didn’t scare. And now here we are, standing on top of what should’ve stayed buried.”

Clara held her breath, hand tight around the lantern handle. Jonas’s fingers brushed against hers, steadying, silent.

"We lost Maddox because of this place," Crane continued. "We've lost others. Fee's had to clean it up more than once. Thought it was over. Thought we could keep the past shut tight."

A long pause. Then, quieter:

"You think I like working for him? You think I don't hate what this town became?"

Jonas moved then, just a footfall, silent. He angled toward the far side of the hollow chamber, counting the beam bracings, looking for another way out. No trap like this was built with only one door.

Above them, Crane sighed.

"You should've left it alone."

Another set of footsteps crunched up behind him.

Two more men. Jonas caught the scrape of a shovel head. A lantern being lit.

Clara's grip tightened.

"We're not going to hurt you," Crane said. "But Fee says you can't leave. Not until we know what you found."

Clara leaned toward Jonas, whispering barely above a breath: "There's another exit."

Jonas nodded once. He'd seen it too, a low vent near the back wall, likely for airflow. Just wide enough.

Behind them, Crane's lantern flared. Light spilled down the stairs, golden and flickering.

Jonas motioned to Clara: go.

She slipped toward the wall, silent as snowfall. Jonas followed, breath steady, heart hammering in his chest like a misfired piston.

Voices above again.

"Did you hear that?" one of the men asked.

Crane moved closer. The ladder creaked beneath him.

Clara pulled aside a bracing plank at the back wall. The earth beyond was narrow, close, but open. A root cellar tunnel, probably dug years ago, an old exit. She slipped through it, and Jonas followed close behind.

The tunnel curved. Earth crumbled. The scent of rot and iron grew stronger.

Behind them, boots hit the floor of the chamber. Crane's voice echoed, low and wary:

"Where the hell did they go?"

Then the sound of crates being moved.

Jonas and Clara crawled, hands pressed into cold clay, shoulders brushing root and stone. After what felt like hours, the tunnel opened up; a shallow outlet behind a ridge, obscured by a fallen tree and a tangle of brush.

They burst into the daylight together, lungs heaving, snow on their shoulders. Jonas stood first, scanning the woods.

No one in sight.

Clara turned, brushing mud from her knees, voice shaking not from fear, but from fury.

"They knew. All of them. They've known for years."

Jonas nodded, eyes still fixed on the clearing. "We just proved it."

And deep in the woods, behind the hollow tree, Crane's voice rose once more, shouting now.

But it was too late. They were already gone.

Chapter 9 – Beneath the Frost

November 8, 1895 — Blowville

They didn't speak for the first mile back.

The woods behind them, dense, still, and indifferent, seemed to swallow sound. Snow clung to their coats. Clara's skirts were soaked to the knee, and Jonas's boots had picked up so much mud and pine debris that every step pulled at him like a weight.

Only when the roofs of Blowville came into view, smoke rising soft from chimneys, dogs barking in far-off yards, did Clara finally speak.

"They were going to trap us down there."

Jonas didn't answer at first. He looked at her, then past her, toward the ridge they'd escaped from just that morning.

"They didn't expect us to find the back exit," he said. "They expected that door to close. Permanently."

She nodded. "They didn't just cover up deaths. They buried them."

They arrived at Elmer's workshop just after noon. The air smelled of sawdust and coal oil, the door half open despite the cold. Elmer stood at his bench, planing a length of maple that would become a bed frame for the new boarding house. He looked up when they entered, one glance told him everything.

Without a word, he locked the door behind them.

"You found it," he said.

"We found something," Jonas replied. "A cellar below the clearing. Hidden for a long time. Crates of papers, a badge. Evidence someone tried to hide."

Elmer set the plane down. Wiped his hands on a rag. "Crane?"

Jonas nodded. "Came after us with two men. Thought he could scare us into silence."

"Didn't work," Clara said. Her voice had sharpened. "We have proof now. Names. Dates. Symbols. Even a second name tag, someone who died after Maddox."

Elmer motioned them to the table in the back corner of the shop. A woodstove glowed in the corner, giving off the kind of heat that soaked into the bones. He poured three cups of strong, bitter coffee. None of them needed sugar.

They sat.

For a long time, no one spoke.

Then Elmer said, "You know what happens next, don't you?"

Jonas looked at him. "Fee doubles down. Makes someone disappear again."

Clara nodded. "And the longer we wait, the more he has time to burn what's left."

She pulled her journal from her satchel and opened to the latest page. It was half full already, maps, notations, sketches of the Freck symbols, transcriptions of what she'd seen carved into the hollow tree's walls.

"I'm going to copy every record," she said. "Everything I've written since the first marking I saw. And I'm going to send one set to the Cameron County paper. Another to Coudersport. Maybe even Philadelphia."

"That's dangerous," Elmer said.

"Good," she replied.

Jonas ran a hand through his hair. "We need more than words. We need witnesses. Names. Someone who saw Fee order a cover-up. Or saw what happened to Maddox, or Ebenspecker."

"I might know one," Elmer said, slowly. "An old teamster. Silas Burke. Lives near Costello now. He hauled bark off the Freck back in '86. Said he saw something... wouldn't ever tell me what."

Clara closed the journal and tucked it under her arm. "Then we go to Costello."

"Not we," Elmer said. "Not yet. You two stay here. Rest. Let the fire warm your bones and let Fee think you're rattled."

He pulled on his coat and opened the door. "I'll go to Silas."

Clara looked at Jonas. Then back at Elmer. "Be careful."

He gave her a crooked smile. "I'm too old to be careful. But I'm just young enough to be useful."

He left into the snow without another word.

Clara stood by the stove, turning slowly in place, eyes distant.

"Do you think the town knows?" she asked quietly.

"I think the town remembers," Jonas said. "Even if it doesn't speak."

And outside, as snow whispered down and the shadows lengthened over Blowville's rooftops, a hush seemed to settle, thicker than before. Like the land itself was listening.

Waiting.

Chapter 10 – Tannin and Iron

November 9, 1895 — Blowville

Terrence Fee stood alone in the upper vat room of the bark mill, watching the steam coil upward through broken slats in the ceiling. The smell of tannin was overwhelming, sharp, metallic, and sour, but he preferred it here.

It helped him think.

Below, men moved like ants around the drying racks. Wagons came and went. The furnace clanged as it was stoked for the afternoon boil. Blowville kept turning, unaware, or pretending not to be aware, that control was slipping.

They'd gotten out. Jonas and Clara.

He'd read Crane's note twice before burning it in the stove.

They escaped. Used the old tunnel. Took papers.

Fee didn't curse. He didn't throw things. That wasn't his way. But he poured himself a glass of rye with a shaking hand, and when the door behind him creaked open without a knock, he turned with eyes like sharpened glass.

Crane stood in the doorway, hat in hand, face pale from the cold or shame, Fee couldn't tell.

"We didn't know about the back passage," Crane said. "I swear it."

Fee said nothing.

"They were fast. Slipped out through the root line. We didn't catch them, but we cleared the cellar. Burned what we couldn't carry."

"You burned the badge?" Fee asked, voice low.

Crane hesitated. "We..."

“Don’t lie to me.”

Crane straightened his shoulders. “No. We didn’t. Jonas has it.”

Fee turned away. The steam hissed behind him. The vat’s surface bubbled like something alive.

“You’ve served me well, Crane,” Fee said quietly. “But if this girl sends her scribbles to the county paper… if some clerk in Coudersport puts together the Freck deaths with the Maddox name tag and the survey symbols…” He trailed off.

Crane cleared his throat. “It’s not too late. Webber’s a loner. He can be bought, or disappeared. Same with the girl.”

Fee raised a hand.

“No more accidents. No more creek drownings. It’s too messy now.”

He walked to the window overlooking the town. Snow blanketed the rooftops, softening the angles, but not the truths beneath.

“We do it quiet,” he said. “We discredit them. Make it look like grief. Madness. Two young minds too full of stories. Maybe a fire. Maybe something... unfortunate.”

Crane shifted. “And what about Fields? He’s helping them. I saw them together.”

Fee’s jaw flexed.

“Elmer’s a craftsman, not a fighter. He’s spent too long bending wood. He’ll bend to pressure.”

Fee turned back toward Crane, his expression calm but stripped of warmth.

“Have one of the boys visit him. Remind him how easy it is to lose fingers around the planer.”

Crane nodded, slowly.

"And the cellar?" he asked.

Fee poured another glass. "Seal it. Again. This time with stone, as it was before."

He downed the rye in one swallow, throat tight.

"The woods have served us for a long time," he said. "But the trees have roots, Crane. And those roots run deeper than bark and deeper than truth."

He walked toward the door, boots thudding softly on the timber floor.

"Make sure no one else sees what they saw," he said. "Or the next tree that falls won't be in the forest. It'll be this town."

Chapter 11 – The Road to Costello

November 10, 1895 — On the Crosscut Trail

The road to Costello wasn't a road at all in November.

It was a frozen trail of rutted mud, pine roots, and ice patches slick as glass. Elmer Fields walked it anyway, coat cinched tight, scarf tucked high over his ears. He carried a pack slung over one shoulder, and in the inside pocket of his wool coat, folded carefully between a ledger page and a square of oilcloth, was the survey map with the circle.

He hadn't taken a trip like this in years. Not since the old days when he'd hauled lumber between townships before Blowville had roofs and men like Fee had deeds.

Snow flurried sideways as he walked. The sky hung low, gray and pressed tight to the hills.

By late afternoon, he reached the edge of Costello.

It looked much like Blowville had looked eight years ago, lean-to sheds, a tannery that coughed black smoke, a store with barrels out front, and a logging camp half-built along the east ridge. The First Fork curled around the edge of town, thick with ice.

He asked around quietly, careful not to draw attention. Most people didn't question him; a man with rough hands and a steady face could pass anywhere in lumber country.

By dusk, he found the cabin.

Silas Burke's place sat on the edge of the woods, past the tannery, its roof low and dark beneath a bent pine. Smoke rose thin from the chimney. A mule stood dozing in a lean-to beside the porch, its harness slung and dry.

Elmer knocked twice.

Nothing.

He knocked again. Then, a shuffle of boots, a click of metal, and the door opened a crack.

Silas Burke peered out, grizzled, half-blind in one eye, with a white scar curling down his temple like a rivulet.

"Elmer Fields?" the man rasped. "Well, I'll be damned. You're supposed to be buried under bark by now."

"Not yet," Elmer said with a faint smile. "But I'm closer than I like."

Burke stepped back. "Come in, then. If you've come all this way, it ain't for conversation."

Inside was warm, though dim. A fire snapped in the hearth. The place smelled of boiled coffee and old wool. A rifle rested on hooks above the door. A whittled bear sat on the mantle.

"I'm here about the Freck," Elmer said, lowering his pack.

Burke's face didn't change, but his shoulders tensed.

"I told you years ago, I don't speak on that."

"I know," Elmer said. "But things have changed."

He pulled the survey map from his coat, laid it flat on the table. Pointed to the circle. The mark they now knew wasn't just a warning, but a seal.

Burke stared at it for a long time.

"Still thought about it, you know," he said, voice quieter now. "All these years. What I saw."

"Then tell it."

Burke looked toward the fire.

"I was hauling bark from the bottom of the Freck. Maddox

was ahead of me on the trail. He went off-path for a smoke. Didn't come back."

Elmer said nothing.

"I waited. Called. Thought he might've wandered down to the run. Then I heard a scream. I went looking, I saw where he'd stepped into the clearing."

Burke's eyes went distant.

"It wasn't empty, then. There was a building there, low to the ground, stone and timber. He was at the door."

"What happened?" Elmer asked.

Burke's hand trembled slightly as he poured a splash of whiskey into his coffee.

"He went in. I waited. Maybe five minutes. Then I heard him scream again. Loud. But not like pain. Like, like he'd seen something he'd been carrying his whole life. And then he was gone. I went down. Looked inside. Empty."

"Empty?"

Burke nodded.

"No sign of Maddox. Just scratch marks on the walls. Symbols. That circle."

He took a long drink.

"I never hauled another load from that side of the Freck again."

Elmer folded the map carefully.

"Jonas Webber and Clara Moran found it again," he said. "It's open."

Burke's eyes sharpened. "Then you'd best tell them what I didn't back then."

“What’s that?”

“That the woods don’t just hold secrets. They keep accounts.”

He stood slowly, reached for a bundle tucked high on the hearth. Pulled out a leather notebook, worn, singed at the edges.

“I got this from Maddox the day he vanished,” he said. “He was writing and drawing in it for months prior.”

He handed it to Elmer.

“Now I think you’re the one meant to read it.”

Outside, the wind picked up. Snow fell heavier now, sliding in through the cracks of the world.

Elmer tucked the journal into his coat.

Tomorrow, he would head back to Blowville.

And with him, he would carry the voice of a man lost to time, and the words that might finally burn Fee’s silence to the ground.

* * *

Elmer left Costello before sunrise.

The storm had passed in the night, but the cold had deepened behind it. Snow lay in sharp, dry crusts across the high ridges, and the First Fork, wide and black in the daylight, moved with the sluggish reluctance of winter coming early.

He followed the old woodsman’s trail south, the same path he’d used decades ago when hauling saw blades and pitch barrels between towns. His legs ached more now. The cold crept deeper into his knees. But he moved with purpose, one hand always resting near the inside pocket of his coat where Maddox’s journal now rode.

He'd only flipped through a few pages the night before, just enough to know the contents weren't idle ramblings. Maddox had written like a man trying to outrun his own mind. Notes on trees that bled without being cut. Men who walked into the Freck and came back with different voices. A drawing of the same symbol Clara had been tracing for weeks.

"It's not the woods," Maddox had scrawled on one page. "It's what's beneath them. Something we woke up when we peeled too deep."

Around midday, Elmer stopped at a rise that overlooked the winding path below, a bend in the First Fork, where the water curved like a question mark around a bluff of stone. He had a memory here. Hauling beams with Silas Burke. They'd eaten lunch on that very ridge, laughing about something, he couldn't even remember what.

The silence now was total.

Too total.

He turned, just as a shadow moved behind the trees.

Elmer froze.

A figure stood at the edge of the trail. Not moving. Not speaking.

Just... watching.

Bundled in a dark coat, scarf drawn high, face lost in shade. The only feature Elmer could make out was the broadness of the man's shoulders, and the unmistakable glint of a shovel head slung across his back.

Fee's man.

Elmer didn't speak. He didn't run either.

He simply adjusted the strap on his shoulder and kept walking, slow and deliberate, like he hadn't seen a thing.

The figure didn't follow.

But he knew, he was being tracked.

It took him five more hours to reach the edge of Blowville.

By the time he saw the first plumes of chimney smoke rising between the bare limbs of the hillside, his beard was stiff with ice and the joints in his hands had begun to lock.

He knocked on Clara Moran's door just before dusk.

Jonas answered, lantern in hand, looking ten years older than he had three days ago.

"Did you find him?" Jonas asked.

Elmer nodded, stepped inside, and unwrapped his coat. He pulled the journal from beneath his shirt and set it gently on the table beside Clara's ledger.

"He saw it," Elmer said. "The cellar. The mark. The scream."

Clara stood across from him, her face pale and still.

Jonas sat down slowly, eyes fixed on the journal.

"And now?"

Elmer looked at them both.

"Now you write it down. All of it. Before someone makes you disappear like they did to Maddox."

From the dark outside, the wind rose like a voice through the eaves.

And in the distance, up where the Freck warrant loomed above Blowville, a tree cracked in the cold, and fell without warning.

Chapter 12 – Ink and Ash

November 11, 1895 — Blowville

The stove crackled softly in the corner of the Moran home, casting long amber shadows across the table where Clara and Jonas worked side by side. Pages were spread in every direction, her journal, the old survey map, Maddox's torn and smoke-scented notebook, and a fresh sheaf of linen paper, crisp and waiting.

Clara dipped her pen and began copying.

"Maddox. Disappeared spring of '87. Last seen by Silas Burke entering the hollow clearing at the bottom of the Freck tract. Screamed once. Never came out."

Jonas leaned over a crate nearby, organizing items they could physically prove: the constable's badge, the metal tag from the tree roots, a charcoal rubbing of the "BELOW" carving inside the hollow hemlock. He paused over each item, checking their placement like a puzzle that refused to align.

"We have facts," he said. "But people don't trust facts anymore. Not in towns like this."

"They trust stories," Clara replied without looking up. "Which is why we'll give them both."

She set down the pen and picked up Maddox's journal again. Its pages were darker now, more ragged the deeper she went. Some entries were little more than scratches. Others were frantic, sketched symbols in the margins, fragments of names: *Fee*, *Crane*, even *W.H. Moran*.

She paused. Looked up.

"My father's name is in here."

Jonas turned. "Where?"

She showed him the page.

It was just a line, half-finished.

"Talked to Moran today. Doesn't believe me. Thinks it's just rot in the beams. But I saw the way he looked at the map. He knows where the seal is."

Clara stared at the ink until it blurred.

"He never told me," she said. "Never once."

Jonas sat down beside her. "Maybe he was trying to protect you."

"Or protect himself."

They sat in silence for a while, the fire softening the edges of their thoughts.

Eventually, Clara stood and walked to the window. The snow had stopped, but Blowville had turned gray again, like the sky had dropped a lid over the town. A team of oxen passed on the road below. Somewhere farther down, a dog barked. And near the pig's ear, smoke curled upward from a chimney that hadn't been used in days.

She turned back.

"I'm going to send these pages out," she said. "Not just to the *Potter Enterprise*. I'll send a set to the *Harrisburg Patriot*, maybe even *Philadelphia Inquirer* if I can get it there."

"That'll make you a target," Jonas said quietly.

"I already am."

He didn't argue.

She handed him the first copy, ten pages long now, carefully written, signed at the bottom in firm black ink: *Clara Moran, Blowville, PA.*

"You're not going to sign it?" she asked.

Jonas shook his head. "I'm the scaleman. No one trusts a man who measures wood for a living."

"But they might believe one who came back from the hollow alive."

He held her gaze. Then, slowly, he reached for a second page and signed: *Jonas Webber, Freck warrant scaler, 1895*

Clara nodded. "We deliver these tomorrow. Before anyone else disappears."

Just then, a sound outside, a quiet knock at the side door. Not the front. Not the porch.

Jonas was already on his feet.

He drew back the curtain.

No one stood there.

But a single object had been left on the step.

Clara opened the door with careful hands.

A freshly peeled strip of hemlock bark, curled like a scroll.

And burned into it, deep and uneven:

"STOP DIGGING"

* * *

The bark warning lay in the cold ashes of the stove now, crackling as the fire slowly consumed it.

Jonas had wanted to keep it. Clara had insisted on burning it. *"It's not a message,"* she said. *"It's a leash. And I won't carry their threats like a collar."*

They dressed in silence, layering coats and scarves against the early winter bite. Clara tucked the envelope inside her journal, which she wrapped in waxed cloth and tied with twine. Jonas checked the weight of the constable's badge in his coat pocket. A symbol, maybe, or a relic. Either way, it had a place in what they were about to do.

Outside, the town seemed quieter than usual.

Men moved down the street in pairs. No one lingered. No children played near the mill road. The only real sound was the dull clatter of hooves from a cart dragging strips of bark to the drying yard.

They passed the general store without looking in. Passed the pig's ear without slowing. A man leaned on the porch rail with a cigarette, watching them, not with recognition, but with assessment.

"He's watching for Crane," Jonas muttered.

Clara didn't answer. She walked straight-backed, eyes forward.

The post office sat on the north end of Main Street, tucked between the old schoolhouse and the tannery manager's office. Smoke rose from its chimney. A fresh stack of crates had just been unloaded from the incoming wagon, parcels bound for Coudersport, Galeton, and farther.

They stepped inside.

Warmth and cedar oil wrapped around them. Behind the counter stood Ira Shelburn, the postmaster, half-blind, hard of hearing, and loyal to no one but his timetables.

Clara approached the counter. She placed the envelope down firmly.

"This needs to go out with the afternoon dispatch."

Shelburn squinted, then reached for his wire-frame glasses. "Name?"

"Clara Moran," she said. "And Jonas Webber."

"Destination?"

She slid a second envelope across the counter. "One to *The Potter Enterprise*. One to *The Harrisburg Patriot*. Both marked personal and urgent."

Shelburn frowned at the seal. "Something wrong, Miss Moran?"

"Yes," she said. "And if these don't go out, you'll be the man who stopped the story from being told."

That gave him pause.

Jonas leaned closer. "Just send them, Ira."

Shelburn nodded and slid the envelopes into his outbox.

Outside, the wind picked up, sharp and cold down the length of the street. Clouds were building again over the ridgeline. Snow by morning.

Clara and Jonas turned toward the road.

The town watched them as they walked back.

No one said a word.

Chapter 13 – Quiet Law

November 11, 1895 (evening) — Blowville

Sheriff Horace Farnsworth lit his pipe three times before it held.

He sat alone in the back room of the jailhouse, staring through a window smeared with soot and early frost. The flame from the lantern flickered against the wall, casting his shadow long across the plank floor.

He'd received the word an hour ago.

A boy, one of Fee's errand runners, had passed it on without much ceremony: *"The girl sent pages. Two of them. Post office."*

Farnsworth had said nothing. Just nodded. Then walked back to his chair and sat down like a man settling into a deeper sort of silence.

It had finally happened.

They weren't whispering anymore.

Clara Moran and Jonas Webber had broken the rule that kept Blowville from tearing itself apart. They'd named things. Drawn lines. Sent truth outside the hollow where it couldn't be buried.

And now... he would have to choose.

He looked across the room to the narrow shelf where he kept the town's ledgers: incident reports, land claims, property disputes, payroll thefts, one forgotten warrant for a drifter who never came back.

Not one word in those books about Maddox.

Not one mention of George Ebenspecker's wound.

And not a single line about the carved circle that he himself had seen, many times, up on the Freck.

He took the pipe from his mouth, exhaled slowly. Smoke drifted toward the ceiling beams.

A knock at the outer door startled him.

He rose, hand near the revolver on his belt, not out of fear, but from habit. He crossed the floor and opened it just enough to see Deputy Stevens standing on the porch, hat in hand, boots wet with slush.

“She really did it,” Stevens said quietly. “Sent both packets. I watched Shelburn put them in the dispatch crate myself.”

Farnsworth opened the door wider. Let him in.

“Fee’ll make a move soon,” the deputy said. “You know that.”

“I do.”

“You gonna stop him?”

Farnsworth walked to the stove, stirred the coals with the iron hook, and didn’t answer right away.

“Fee’s like the trees,” he said finally. “Too big to cut down all at once. You chip away at him, you lose your axe before you hit the heartwood.”

Stevens took a seat. “And if we do nothing?”

Farnsworth looked over.

“Then we watch this town eat another generation.”

He reached into his desk drawer and pulled out a folded slip of paper, one that had been tucked between property maps for nearly a decade. He unfolded it carefully.

Freck warrant – open tract marked in 1884. Report of

screams near hollow tree. Entry sealed. Symbol present – circle/four lines. Initials: H.F.

"I kept this," he said. "Didn't know why then. Maybe I do now."

Stevens leaned forward. "You're going to side with them?"

Farnsworth nodded once. "I'm going to stop pretending I don't already."

Outside, wind cut through the alleys. Somewhere down by the mill, a lantern shattered, whether by accident or intent, Farnsworth couldn't tell.

He stood, took down his coat, and buckled his holster.

"I'll go see Fee myself," he said.

"You sure that's smart?"

"No," Farnsworth replied. "But it's the only thing I haven't tried."

He stepped into the dark, leaving the door open just long enough for cold to slip inside and settle over the maps like dust.

* * *

The Fee Brothers office was dark from the outside, but Farnsworth knew better than to think it was empty.

He crossed the muddy yard behind the bark mill, boots sucking at the ground with each step. Smoke still curled from the chimney, soft and steady, like breath through gritted teeth. The snow had started again, light but sharp, carried by a wind that smelled of wet timber and tannin.

He knocked once.

Then let himself in.

Inside, warmth clung to the walls. Oil lamps burned low, casting flickering shadows across ledgers, crates, and a roll-top desk built with the kind of precision Blowville rarely saw anymore.

Terrence Fee sat behind it.

He didn't rise. Didn't smile. Just poured two fingers of rye into a glass and slid it across the desk toward the empty chair.

"I wondered how long it'd take you," Fee said.

Farnsworth didn't sit. He didn't touch the glass.

"You sent men after them."

Fee shrugged. "You send dogs into the woods, you expect barking."

Farnsworth stared. "You sent them into a hole with no plan but silence. That's not bark. That's a burial."

Fee leaned back in his chair, expression unreadable.

"They're meddling with things that don't concern them. Old things. Dangerous ones."

"They concern me now," Farnsworth said. "They concern the county when death shows up in the creek with an axe wound and a blank report."

"You're not paid to chase ghosts," Fee replied.

"No," Farnsworth said. "But I'm tired of guarding your secrets with my silence."

He reached into his coat and set a folded slip of paper on the desk.

Fee didn't move to read it.

"I saw the symbol too," the sheriff said. "Back in '86. I just didn't write it in the official log. Thought I was protecting the town. Turns out I was just protecting your hold on it."

Fee's lips twitched, nearly a smile.

"You think the truth will fix anything? You think the county will care about a few dead woodsmen and a girl with a journal?"

"I think," Farnsworth said slowly, "you've forgotten what happens when people stop fearing the dark. They start lighting fires."

Fee stood now, slowly.

Behind him, the wind groaned against the windowpanes.

"We built this town," he said. "On timber, yes. On bark. On blood. But it stood. It gave men wages and women roofs. And it kept the wolves at the edge of the trees."

"You are the wolf, Terrence."

Fee leaned in slightly, voice like a blade being drawn.

"If you side with them, you don't walk out of here with a badge. You walk out as a target."

Farnsworth didn't blink.

"I walked in that way."

He turned, coat swinging at his sides, boots echoing across the floor. He paused at the door.

"Clara's not backing down," he said. "Neither is Webber. And now you've got me to deal with too."

Fee didn't answer.

So Farnsworth opened the door and stepped into the snow.

Behind him, the lamp in the office dimmed, then flared brighter.

* * *

The door clicked shut behind Farnsworth like the slam of a vault.

Terrence Fee stood motionless in the middle of the room, fingers still resting on the rim of the untouched glass. Outside, the snow whispered across the mill roofs, and somewhere down the road, a bell rang once from the boarding house porch.

He didn't move until the lantern on the desk sputtered, throwing a crooked shadow of his own silhouette across the far wall.

Then, finally, he sat.

Not with defeat, but with purpose.

He opened the lower drawer of his desk. Pulled out a leather folder bound with rawhide cord. Inside were a dozen folded pages, contracts, payment logs, and signed affidavits, many dated years before Blowville had a name, when the land had just been coordinates and potential.

He set those aside.

What he was looking for was beneath them: a list.

Names. Old and new. Some crossed out in pencil. Others underlined in red.

At the top of the list:
Tramwell (Deserted)
Crane (Trusted – but watch)
H. Farnsworth (Compromised)
C. Moran (Active)
W.H. Moran (No longer a concern)
J. Webber (Unknown – investigate)
E. Fields (Influential – handle carefully)

His jaw clenched.

Fee had always believed control wasn't about force, it was about timing. About pressure applied in the right places. About letting people think they had choices, right until the moment they didn't.

Now he was out of time. The pages were out. The law had turned. And the girl had proven more dangerous than he'd ever anticipated.

He closed the folder and set it in the center of the desk.

Then he rang the bell beside the ledger.

A door opened in the back hallway.

Crane stepped into the light.

Fee didn't look at him when he spoke.

"I want the cellar sealed and gone. I want the whole clearing to vanish under stone."

Crane nodded once. "And the sheriff?"

Fee's voice was cold steel.

"Leave him. For now. But put someone on Fields. And if Jonas or Clara leave town again..."

He looked up.

"No warnings this time."

Crane hesitated. "What if they go to the press? What if the papers run it before we move?"

Fee stood. Walked to the window.

Outside, the snow blurred the line between the trees and the town. Between memory and fire.

"They won't," he said. "Because they still think they're ahead of me."

He turned, slowly.

“And because they haven’t yet learned what Blowville does to people who try to tell the truth.”

Chapter 14 – The Snow Between Us

November 12, 1895 — Blowville

Snow covered the town like a blessing trying to hide a curse.

Fresh powder softened the roofs and fences, muting the sharp corners of Blowville. From the upstairs window of the Moran house, it almost looked peaceful.

But Clara knew better.

She stood at the window. Behind her, her journal lay open, blank. The ink wouldn't flow, not from lack of thought, but from the weight of everything they'd uncovered. Everything they were about to risk.

Jonas sat near the hearth, coiling the cord around the oilskin pouch that held their only copies of the evidence. His silence said enough.

"They haven't come yet," Clara said.

"They will," Jonas replied.

Clara turned. "Do you think they'll go after Elmer?"

"He's the one they didn't plan on. That makes him a problem."

She closed the journal.

"We should've sent more copies. Should've taken them ourselves."

"We still might have to," Jonas said. "If the postmaster's compromised, the letters are ash already."

"I watched him stamp them."

"I've seen stamped ones burned all the same."

He pulled the old constable's badge from his coat pocket

and set it on the table. The metal was cold, but the etching still clear:

PC Constable – 1886

Jonas stared at it. "Maddox must've known it would end badly. He left this as the last piece."

Clara touched it gently. "And Silas remembered. That was enough. Maybe it still is."

Jonas looked up. "You still believe that? That truth matters here?"

"Yes," she said. "Because if we stop believing that, then what are we even fighting for?"

A knock broke the quiet.

Three sharp raps.

Jonas stood fast, peered through the curtain.

"Just a boy," he said. "Tanner's apprentice."

Clara opened the door.

The boy, no older than twelve, held out a folded paper. "He told me to give this to you. Said not to read it until you were inside."

"Who?" she asked.

The boy hesitated. "Didn't say. Limped. Looked mean."

She closed the door, unfolded the note. The handwriting was unmistakably her father's.

"They know about the journal. Elmer's shop burned last night. I drew them to the house, made them think I had the papers. I'm meeting Elmer at the log slide at dusk. Come alone. Bring nothing."

She read it twice.

Jonas was already standing.

“It’s a trap.”

“Maybe,” she said. “Or maybe it’s the only way to get Elmer out before they disappear him like Maddox.”

She reached for her cloak.

“I’m not going alone.”

Jonas nodded. “Then we go.”

She slipped the journal into her satchel. The badge into her glove.

The snow fell quiet as they stepped into the street.

Each shuttered window they passed felt like it watched.

* * *

Elmer Fields moved along the ridge trail like a man who knew the weight of being followed.

The slope above Blowville was slick with snowmelt and old bark. The log slide, long since abandoned, curved downhill like a scar left too long unhealed.

He reached the clearing and waited.

The wind murmured through the trees.

They’d burned his workshop. Left nothing but scorched beams and a half-melted grindstone. No explanation. Just a warning: You were seen.

He didn’t trust the note, even if it was in William Moran’s hand.

A crunch of snow to the left.

Elmer turned.

William emerged from the trees, cloak tight around his frame. He looked tired, but unhurt.

"You came," William said.

"Didn't think I'd see you again," Elmer replied.

"They tried last night. Two of Fee's boys. Left oil by the siding. I made sure they saw me burning papers at the hearth."

"You gave them a show."

"I gave them a distraction."

"She knows," Elmer said. "Clara. She's pieced it together."

"She was never meant to get this deep."

"She's deeper than any of us ever were," Elmer said. "And smarter."

William looked toward the trees.

"She's coming, isn't she?"

"She won't let this end with silence."

A sound behind them. Crunching snow.

Three men emerged from the treeline, dark coats, heavy boots. One with a rifle, another with a crowbar.

Fee's men.

William went still.

"I bought you time," he said quietly. "It's all I could manage."

The tallest man stepped forward. "You've got something doesn't belong to you."

Elmer pulled the journal from inside his coat.

“No,” he said. “I’ve got what you tried to bury.”

The rifle lifted.

From the ridge: “Drop it!”

Clara.

Jonas behind her, revolver drawn.

“You can kill us,” Clara called, “but you can’t stop what’s already gone. It’s been sent. Every page.”

Silence.

Then, slowly, the rifle lowered.

Fee’s men backed into the trees, watching Clara like she was more danger than they could name.

Jonas moved to Elmer. “You alright?”

Elmer nodded.

William looked at Clara. There was pride in his eyes, and sorrow.

“You shouldn’t have followed.”

She stepped between the trees.

“We never stopped.”

Chapter 15 – Cracks in the Frost

November 13, 1895 — Blowville

The sun rose reluctantly.

It broke across Blowville's rooftops in weak, watery light, glinting off half-frozen puddles and eaves sagging with icicles. The snow from the night before had crusted, the wind having packed it hard enough to walk across without sinking.

But the stillness felt different now. Not peaceful; expectant.

In the Moran house, Clara stood barefoot in the kitchen, waiting for the kettle to whistle. She hadn't slept, not really. After the log slide, she'd stayed up late, scribbling new pages by candlelight, copying Maddox's words by hand. There was no guarantee the envelopes had made it out of town. She had to assume this, her version, might be the only one that survived.

Across the room, Jonas sat at the table, boots unlaced, reading through a stack of copied letters from the journal. His shirt was torn at one cuff, his knuckles still bruised from when he'd punched the tree in frustration after Fee's men walked away.

"They'll come again," he said softly.

"I know."

He looked up. "You still want to go public?"

Clara didn't hesitate. "That was never a question."

The kettle began to sing.

She poured the water, then turned to the window.

Outside, a figure trudged down Main Street, Sheriff Farnsworth, scarf tight to his neck, coat buttoned high. He stopped briefly at the post office, spoke to the clerk, then turned and walked directly toward the Moran house.

Jonas stood.

"Do you want me to…?"

Clara shook her head. "No. Let him come."

Moments later, the sheriff's knock echoed through the house. Steady. Three raps.

Clara opened the door.

Farnsworth's face was red from the cold, his eyes heavy. He removed his hat.

"May I come in?"

She stepped aside without a word.

He nodded to Jonas as he entered. "Webber."

Jonas didn't reply. Just watched.

Farnsworth stood near the fire, warming his hands.

"Fee's quiet this morning," he said. "Too quiet. Crane's not been seen. Office is shuttered. Men are jumpy."

"Means he's planning something," Jonas said.

"Maybe," Farnsworth said. "Or maybe he knows it's too late."

Clara moved closer. "Did the letters get out?"

Farnsworth turned.

"I stayed up half the night in Shelburn's office. Checked the crate myself. Both your envelopes were still there... until about five minutes before the wagon left town."

Her heart stopped.

"Gone?"

"No," he said. "Delivered. I put them on the wagon myself."

Jonas stepped forward. "So it's done."

Farnsworth shook his head.

"It's started."

Clara looked toward the window again, the pale light pouring through lace curtains like breath.

The silence in Blowville was beginning to crack. And underneath it, voices long buried had begun to stir.

The journal sat open on the table. Maddox's handwriting. Clara's script beneath it. New ink. Old ghosts.

Outside, a bell rang at the tannery.

Not an alarm. Just routine.

But it sounded different now.

* * *

Once Sheriff Farnsworth had gone, the silence returned, but it wasn't the same.

It was a silence laced with momentum. Not dread, but decision.

Clara cleared the table. Jonas stood at the window, watching the path down toward the mill, his hand still wrapped around the handle of the badge in his coat pocket.

"He'll try to close the hollow," Jonas said. "Bury it again before anyone else can find it."

"We knew he would," Clara replied, drying her hands with a

cloth. “That’s why we copied everything. That’s why we sent the letters.”

Jonas turned from the window. “The seal, the one under the tree. If we’re right about it being more than a symbol... if it marks something deeper?”

“Then someone needs to see it before Fee erases it forever,” Clara finished. “Someone outside this place. Someone who can make it matter.”

Jonas nodded. “You thinking what I’m thinking?”

Clara’s mouth tilted into the faintest smile. “That depends. Are you thinking of stealing Fee’s own wagon?”

Jonas blinked. Then smiled back. “I was just thinking of walking out of town.”

“Well,” she said, grabbing her cloak, “my way is faster.”

* * *

They reached the north depot barn by midday.

Fee’s freight wagons sat idle in the yard, hitched to a team of sturdy bays. Snow crunched beneath their boots as they passed the hay pens and ducked through the back gate.

Clara moved with purpose. Her face was red from the wind, but her eyes were clear.

“Fields told me about this wagon,” she said. “Used for private timber inspections. Fee hasn’t taken it since August. It’s got a sealed box under the bench. Reinforced for maps and ledgers.”

“Which we now own,” Jonas said, tightening the last of the harness straps.

They loaded everything: the original journal, the survey map, the rubbings, and a freshly copied set of notes labeled

Property of Clara Moran & Jonas Webber — to be opened if found dead.

Jonas double-checked the buckles. Clara swung into the seat.

She looked at him. "We don't ride all the way to Harrisburg."

"No," Jonas said. "Head north to Coudersport. That's where the first reporter is."

"And the safest set of eyes."

They paused once more, looking back.

Blowville sat quiet under the snow. The mill's chimney smoked. Men walked the muddy tracks near the pig's ear, boots sinking into thaw.

But something had changed. And the town knew it.

As they rolled the wagon onto the north road, a few heads turned.

Not many. But enough.

* * *

Terrence Fee stood at the corner window of his office, hands folded behind his back, watching the sky turn the color of old steel.

Something was wrong.

He couldn't hear it, exactly. But he could feel it.

The mill crew was working half-speed. No shouting. No arguments. Even the dogs seemed to move quieter along the yards. That kind of stillness only meant one thing in Blowville: people knew something and weren't saying it.

He turned to Crane, who stood by the stove, smoking like the flame inside him had started to gutter.

“Where’s the north wagon?” Fee asked, flat.

Crane blinked. “Last I heard, still in the barn.”

“Go check.”

Crane didn’t argue. Just grabbed his coat and went.

Fee walked to his desk, opened the logbook again.

The letter from Farnsworth, refusing his silence, still burned in his mind. The girl’s journal. Webber’s badge. The confrontation at the log slide. All of it was supposed to be over. Controlled. Folded neatly back into the silence.

But something had come loose.

Outside, the door slammed open.

Crane reappeared, breathing hard, snow on his coat.

“They’re gone.”

Fee didn’t speak.

“Took the private wagon. The bay team. Left north, maybe an hour ago.”

“Who saw?”

Crane hesitated. “One of the yard boys.”

Fee nodded once. His voice came quiet and slow.

“They think they can run,” he said.

He walked to the rack above the desk and pulled down his coat, the heavy one lined with boiled leather. The one he hadn’t worn since the war. He buckled the strap at his throat. “They think the truth travels faster than me.”

Crane said nothing.

Fee looked out the window once more, snow falling soft against the glass.

“Then let’s prove them wrong.”

Chapter 16 – The North Road

November 13, 1895 (late afternoon) — Between Blowville and Wharton Fork

The road north unraveled like a scar beneath a blanket of white.

The bay team moved steady, heads low, breath steaming in the cold. Jonas handled the reins with practiced ease, while Clara sat beside him, cloak drawn tight, one hand resting on the satchel that held the second copy of Maddox's journal and the Freck survey maps.

Behind them, the forest thinned and widened; low ridges, iced creek beds, the scattered trunks of stripped hemlock long since felled. The sound of the mill was gone now. So was the weight of Blowville pressing in on their shoulders.

For the first time in days, they breathed easy.

For a while.

"I keep expecting to hear hooves behind us," Clara said, eyes scanning the road behind.

"You won't," Jonas replied. "Not yet."

"You think Fee's still deciding how to handle us?"

Jonas gave her a dry look. "Fee doesn't hesitate. He calculates."

They rode in silence for a stretch.

The trees gave way to a long slope that curved down toward Wharton Fork, a muddy switchback of trail that fed into the Coudersport Pike. A thin river cut through the low valley below, frozen at the edges, but still flowing in its center. Somewhere beyond those trees lay safety. Distance. A printing press with fresh ink.

"How long do we have before he realizes the wagon's missing?" Clara asked.

"Probably already has," Jonas said. "The only question now is what road he takes."

She nodded. "Then we don't stop."

But her voice carried something more than determination now. Regret? Fear? She wasn't sure.

Jonas noticed.

"You thinking about your father?"

She hesitated.

"He tried to help," she said finally. "But I don't know if it was out of guilt or love. I don't know if there's a difference in a town like Blowville."

"There is," Jonas said quietly. "One means you stay. The other means you run to warn someone."

She didn't reply, but her fingers tightened on the satchel.

The sun dipped low, turning the snow blue. The wagon creaked. The horses snorted.

Up ahead, a thin curl of smoke rose from a waystation cabin, abandoned, probably, but still dry if they needed to stop.

Jonas glanced back once more. The road behind them was empty. Still.

But he knew better than to believe it would stay that way.

"We'll make Coudersport by noon tomorrow if the weather holds," he said.

"And if it doesn't?"

He looked at her. His expression was calm. Steady. But in his eyes: readiness. Resolve.

"Then we'll outrun the storm and whatever's riding behind it."

* * *

They saw the flicker of lantern light behind them first.

Just a small glow. Distant. But steady.

Jonas didn't speak.

He reached under the bench and slid the revolver from the holster he'd tied beneath the seat. Checked the cylinder. Five rounds.

Clara stared back at the curve of road, the trees black now against a slate-gray sky.

"How far behind?" she asked.

Jonas looked again. "Half a mile. Maybe less."

They passed the burned-out station cabin and kept moving.

Then; hoofbeats. Not fast. Measured. Professional. Not a posse. Hunters.

Clara looked at Jonas. "They'll catch us before the river bridge."

"I know."

He slowed the wagon. The road was narrowing, flanked by high banks of snow and rock. No room to maneuver. No use outrunning them now.

Instead, he guided the team toward the trees and pulled off onto a game trail, half-buried in drift.

They stopped in a copse of firs, breath rising in clouds.

Jonas jumped down, helped Clara down beside him.

"We hide the satchel," he said.

Clara was already pulling off her glove. "There's a hollow tree, ten feet back. Under the snow."

They moved fast, hands numb, hearts beating high and tight in their throats.

By the time the lanterns rounded the last bend, the satchel was buried beneath a nest of bark and snow-packed moss, just visible if you knew exactly where to look.

And then came the wagon.

Crane was driving.

And beside him, Terrence Fee. Cloaked in black, gloves on, expression like carved granite. There were no guards. No rifles raised. Just two men. And something worse than weapons.

Intent.

Jonas stepped into the road, revolver low at his side.

Clara moved beside him.

Fee raised a hand.

"No need for dramatics," he said, voice calm. "You've made your point."

Clara's voice was clear. "You tried to burn ours."

Fee chuckled. "And yet here you are. Not dead. Not bleeding. Just shivering in the woods like runaways."

Crane held the reins, jaw tight. His eyes flicked to Jonas's revolver, but he made no move.

Fee stepped down from the wagon, boots crunching in the

snow. "You sent letters," he said. "But letters get lost. Roads close. And newspapers lose interest."

Clara didn't move.

"I don't need to kill you," Fee said. "Not if I can make you irrelevant. Not if I can make people think you're delusional. Or dead of exposure. Or drowned in the First Fork trying to flee arrest."

"You wouldn't risk that," Jonas said. "You've already got Sheriff Farnsworth against you."

Fee's smile thinned. "Farnsworth's a tired man. And I've outlived more ambitious enemies."

Jonas cocked the revolver.

Fee didn't flinch.

Then Clara spoke.

"You're not here to stop us," she said. "You're here to see if we're brave enough to keep going."

Fee looked at her, really looked.

She stepped forward. "You've buried bodies. Burned names. Broken families. And you still believe no one will care."

He didn't reply.

Clara pointed back toward the bend in the road.

"We left a trail. You found us. Good. Others will too."

Fee's mouth twitched. Just once.

Then he stepped back and climbed into the wagon.

"Turn around," he told Crane.

Crane looked at him. Surprised.

Fee's voice dropped. "They've already lost. They just don't feel it yet."

And then they were gone.

The wagon rolled back down the road, lanterns dimming into the trees.

Jonas let out a long breath.

Clara turned to him, snow in her hair, her hands shaking from adrenaline and cold.

"You think he meant it?" she asked.

Jonas watched the trees long after the wagon disappeared.

"No," he said. "I think we just bought ourselves time."

He looked at her.

"And we'd better use it."

Chapter 17 – The Water Keeps Secrets

November 13, 1895 (night) — First Fork Crossing

The moon had risen, faint and bone-white, by the time Fee gave the signal.

No words. Just a flick of the hand.

Crane reined the team off the main trail and circled east, following an old skidding path that dipped toward the river. The wheels creaked softly in the frost. Above them, fir branches caught the wind and groaned like old timber.

"We'll hit the crossing in less than a mile," Crane muttered. "They'll be on foot by then. Or still sleeping."

Fee didn't answer.

His eyes were fixed ahead, on the cut of the land and the shadows pooled along the banks of the First Fork. His gloved fingers tapped against his leg in time with the sway of the wagon.

This wasn't anger. This was calculation.

They crested a ridge just above the narrow wooden bridge, half-rotted but still standing, and saw it:

A faint flicker of firelight through the trees. A stopped wagon. Two silhouettes moving near the bank.

Jonas and Clara.

Fee nodded once. Crane drew a long knife from beneath the seat. They moved like men who had done this before.

They left the wagon at the ridge and crept down through the trees. No noise. No wasted motion.

Jonas turned too late.

He was bending near the river, filling a canteen, when the

back of his skull met Crane's hickory club. One blow. Quick. Final.

He collapsed at the edge of the ice, breath clouding once before it stopped.

Clara screamed.

She ran. Fee moved faster.

He caught her near the old flood stump, hands clamping her shoulders, dragging her down into the shallows. Her boots kicked through the mud, fingers clawing at his coat, but Fee was stronger, and colder, and had already made peace with the cost.

She fought until her face broke the ice.

Then the river swallowed her.

Fee stood in the shallows, panting, soaked to the knees. Crane pulled Jonas's body into the water, weighting it with stones pulled from the bank.

They worked in silence, the way only men do when the work is evil and long-rehearsed.

When it was done, they stood on the bank, watching the current pull the story away.

"She was just a girl," Crane said finally.

"No," Fee replied. "She was a voice. And voices echo."

He looked downriver.

"Until they don't."

They mounted the wagon before the sun touched the ridgeline. By the time it did, Clara Moran and Jonas Webber were gone.

And Blowville would wake to the news that the snow had been too much, the river too fast, and two fools had wandered into history without a trace.

That was the version the town would be told.

And for now, it would be enough.

Chapter 18 – The Way Towns Grieve

November 14, 1895 — Blowville

They said the ice cracked beneath them.

That was the version that spread before noon.

By then, the news had reached the cookhouse, the general store, and the pig's ear. It moved fast, quieter than truth, louder than lies. A pair of gloves had been found on the riverbank. A broken lantern, half-frozen in the current. And footprints, faint and unhurried, leading down to the First Fork and never coming back.

The town accepted it like wood accepts a nail.

Clara Moran and Jonas Webber, gone.

Drowned in the dark water north of town. Maybe lost. Maybe trying to flee.

There would be no bodies, not yet. The current would keep them until spring, the old men said. The water always did.

Sheriff Farnsworth sat on the steps of the jailhouse with his pipe clenched and cold.

He didn't move for an hour.

He'd seen the look on Crane's face when the man passed through town that morning. Too blank. Too clean. As if the cold had never touched him. And Fee hadn't come back at all.

Inside, the journal was still locked in the desk drawer. The last copy. The only one not sent. He hadn't opened it since Clara handed it to him days ago, but today he did.

The pages crackled like kindling.

Across town, William Harvey Moran didn't speak to anyone.

He was in his shop when he got the new. He stood by the window for most of the morning, staring out across the yard toward the ridge, where the snow had begun to melt at the edges.

He didn't weep.

He just stood there, one hand flat on the wall, as if feeling for something that had already gone.

* * *

At the mill, men kept working.

Fee had not returned. That was the talk beneath the breath. Some said he was in Coudersport. Others said he was meeting with lawyers in Galeton. No one mentioned the bloodstain behind Crane's right boot. No one asked why his voice cracked when he barked orders near the bark vats.

Blowville continued its strange dance.

No one said the word murder. But no one used the word accident either.

Instead, they said
"Shame."
"Tragic."
"They were too smart for this place."
"She should've stayed out of the woods."

* * *

That night, Elmer Fields stood alone by the clearing behind the old scaler's cabin. He held a lantern in one hand, and in the other, a sheet of paper, wet with snow, black with ink.

He didn't burn it.

He nailed it to the trunk of a pine, just outside the path to the Freck.

The wind tried to tear it away, but it held.

And at the top, in Clara's handwriting, it read:

"There is something beneath the trees. And the trees remember."

* * *

By sundown, snow had begun to fall again.

Soft, wet flakes drifted through the streets and gathered on rooftops, washing the town in a hush that felt more like a blanket than a burial. But not everyone slept.

Inside the jailhouse, Sheriff Farnsworth lit the lamp, locked the front door, and unrolled the survey map Clara had annotated. Beside it, he laid the badge Jonas had once carried. Next to that, the final pages of the journal she had rewritten by hand; names, places, dates, symbols.

The story Fee thought he had buried.

He folded the documents into a brown envelope, sealed it, and inked a name on the front: *R.H. Carver – Coudersport Potter Enterprise*.

He'd ride out with it himself come morning. Alone, if need be.

As the oil in the lamp hissed, he sat down and opened Clara's journal to the first page. Her handwriting was small, deliberate.

"I was born in a town that was never meant to be remembered."

He read on.

Outside, the snow kept falling.

* * *

Two days later, at the edge of the Freck, just beyond where the last tree had been felled, Elmer Fields returned to the marker he'd posted.

The page Clara wrote was already stiff with ice, but still legible.

There is something beneath the trees. And the trees remember.

He added a second page beneath it. His handwriting. Bigger. Cruder.

We remember too.

He pounded in the nail, hard.

Behind him, the woods groaned faintly as wind passed through the canopy. Somewhere in that dark, roots still twisted beneath the soil. But the story had been pulled into the light. Spoken. Sent.

Blowville would go on, as towns like it do.

But it would never again be quiet.

And the truth, like spring thaw, was already moving beneath the surface.

Part Two

Chapter 19 – Death in the Valley

October 1898 — South of Wharton Mills

The cows hadn't been milked, and the stove was cold.

That was the first thing John Mohan noticed when he passed William Ayers's farmhouse just after sunrise. The place was quiet, too quiet for a man who rose with the sun and cursed at the frost. Mohan whistled once. No dog barked.

He paused at the gate. The house leaned just slightly to the east, as it always had, and the windows were dark behind drawn curtains. Smoke should've been rising from the chimney. Instead, the roof was rimmed with frost, hard as bone.

Mohan stepped up onto the porch.

There were bootprints frozen in the mud, but not Ayers's. He could tell by the depth and the stride. He was about to call out again when he saw the ladder, leaned against the side of the porch, angled toward the second-story window.

The same window Ayers had once nailed shut "to keep the wind out and the damned stories in."

Mohan didn't call this time. He climbed the ladder.

Inside, the bedroom was still. The bedclothes were soaked through. The floor was red and black. Ayers was there, but not whole. His jaw was gone, and his eyes were open like they'd been waiting for someone.

Later, people would say he died in his sleep. Others would whisper that someone, or something, pulled him from it.

The sheriff was sent for. The coroner too. And by the time the noon train passed, the story had started to twist.

Some said it was a robbery. Some said it was a woman's revenge. And a few, mostly the old men, mostly the ones who still remembered Clara Moran and what was found under the hollow tree, said it was the woods.

That it had started again.

And that the truth wasn't buried deep enough.

Chapter 20 – Stranger in the Hollow

October 17, 1898 — Blowville

Rebecca Ayers had seen death before.

She had watched it creep through hospitals during the diphtheria surge in Harrisburg, had wrapped bandages around limbs turned gray by infection, had once helped a young boy hold his sister's hand as she slipped into stillness. Death, in the city, was brisk and crowded and unavoidable.

But death in the woods was different.

It lingered.

She stepped off the cart at the edge of Blowville, boots crunching over packed earth and horse dung, her travel bag slung over one shoulder. The driver tipped his hat and turned the wagon back toward the main road without waiting for thanks.

Blowville didn't welcome visitors.

The town lay low in the hollow, crouched along Bailey Run like it had grown from the mud and bark itself. Most of the buildings were grayed with weather and wear. Roofs bowed under moss. Smoke hung low from chimneys, but windows remained shuttered, like eyes refusing to meet hers.

She pulled her coat tighter.

The letter from the sheriff had been brief:
Your uncle, William Ayers, was found deceased. We request a family member settle his estate.

No explanation. No apology.

Rebecca hadn't seen Uncle William in years, not since her father's funeral. He'd been a man of hard angles and harsh words, a bachelor farmer with few attachments and fewer affections. Still, he was blood. And blood called, even when you didn't want it to.

The Ayers farm was three miles southeast, but she had come to town first. She needed the coroner's report. She needed to speak with the sheriff. She needed to see for herself what no one in the letter would say.

At the post office, the clerk looked her over once before thumbing through a stack of papers.

"Letter for you came in from Costello," he muttered. "Said to expect a woman asking questions."

He handed her a note, unsealed.

Rebecca unfolded it. The handwriting was neat. Controlled.

Miss Ayers, I'm sorry for your loss. I would speak with you before you visit the house. There are things you should know. Please come to the carpenter's shop, back of Main Street. Ask for Fields.
— H. Farnsworth

She read it twice.

The name was familiar. *Farnsworth.* The sheriff.

She made her way along the muddy boardwalk past the store, the mill, and the sagging frame of what looked like a saloon. Men stared as she passed, but none spoke. A dog barked once. A bell clanged from the tannery behind the mill yard.

Blowville moved like a machine with no joy in its function.

The carpenter's shop stood quiet behind a row of drying sheds. The sign read E. Fields in faded white paint. She knocked twice.

An old man answered, broad in the shoulders, though stooped now, with hands that had built a town and a face that had buried too many pieces of it.

"Rebecca Ayers?" he asked.

She nodded.

"Come inside, Miss. We've got tea, and you've got ghosts."

* * *

The inside of Elmer Fields' shop smelled of cedar dust and pipe smoke. Tools hung on the walls in precise rows, their wooden handles worn smooth with decades of use. A kettle steamed gently atop a potbelly stove, and beside it, a teacup rested on a stack of saw-cut planks as if it had been waiting just for her.

"Sit, please," Elmer said, gesturing to the bench across from him. "Sheriff asked me to speak with you first."

Rebecca sat, ungloving her fingers and letting them warm against the cup. She took in the space, quiet, clean, lived-in. She'd met men like Elmer in Harrisburg: craftsmen who measured twice, spoke once, and carried their grief in their joints.

She noticed a photograph tucked into the corner of a shelf above the workbench. A young woman, sharp-eyed, standing before a stand of hemlock trees. The name *Clara* was scrawled faintly in pencil beneath the edge.

"My niece," Elmer said softly. "Not by blood. By choice."

Rebecca turned back toward him. "You knew her?"

"I buried her," he said, his voice even. "And her story."

He let the words hang.

Then, without asking permission, he picked up a thin folder from beneath the bench and placed it gently before her.

"This was taken from your uncle's house after they found him. Sheriff didn't want it made public. Thought it best someone tell you in person."

Rebecca opened the folder.

Inside: a small square of wood, smooth as glass, cut from a windowsill. And scratched into it, barely visible beneath the grain, a name:

C. Moran

She looked up sharply. “Clara Moran.”

Elmer nodded.

“She used to write things,” he said. “Truths people didn’t want to read. About this town. About the Freck. About the hollow tree and what was buried beneath it.”

Rebecca blinked. “My uncle never mentioned…”

“He wouldn’t have. He was a quiet man. But not a blind one. That window was in his bedroom.”

She felt a chill that had nothing to do with the air.

“There’s more,” Elmer said. “The morning they found him, the window was open. Frost on the inside. Bootprints in the yard. And someone had drawn this.”

He reached into his coat and handed her another item, a torn scrap of paper, stained with soot and damp.

On it, the same symbol repeated: a circle with four lines, intersecting at angles.

Rebecca had never seen it before.

But something in her gut recoiled.

“What is it?” she asked.

Elmer took a breath. “We don’t know. We just know it means someone’s watching.”

She stared at the scrap, then at the carved name, then at the man.

“Why me?” she asked. “Why tell me this?”

Elmer leaned forward.

“Because you came back. Just like Clara did. And because I think your uncle died trying to remember something the rest of us are still trying to forget.”

Outside, the wind rose, carrying with it the scent of bark smoke and something older.

Rebecca felt the town folding in around her.

She hadn’t come to Blowville for answers.

But something told her she’d leave with more than a grave and a deed.

Chapter 21 – A Map of Silence

October 17, 1898 — Blowville Jailhouse

Sheriff Horace Farnsworth unlocked the bottom drawer of his desk with hands he no longer trusted.

They had grown slower these past five years, stiff at dawn, knotted by noon, but it wasn't just age. It was the weight of what they hadn't done. Of what they'd let be buried.

He sat back as the drawer creaked open.

Inside was a faded envelope, brittle at the corners, marked only with a name: Clara Moran.

He hadn't opened it since the winter of '96, when Fee's boys had "found" her journal pages buried in a snowbank south of Coudersport. Some pages were soaked through. Others had been torn. Only the envelope and the last ten pages had been salvaged.

He pulled them out now and spread them across the desk.

The handwriting was unmistakable. Sharp. Clean. A woman raised by order and ink.

"They think the woods are dead. But they're not. They're dreaming. And they remember who cut them first."

He remembered the night those pages arrived. The ink barely dry. The look on Fee's face when he learned a copy had made it out after all. They'd said it was too late to matter.

But Fee had gone quiet after that winter.

The kind of quiet that meant he was busy making sure it never happened again.

Farnsworth lit the lantern.

He pulled out an old surveyor's map, its corners curling like dried leaves. He flattened it beside the pages. The Freck warrant still loomed in the center, miles of uncut timber, land once claimed, then abandoned.

He marked the hollow tree with a piece of charcoal. Just a dot. Still there. Still sealed.

He'd not been back since the deaths.

Jonas and Clara's bodies were never found. Fee claimed they'd drowned. Crane said the current had taken them. The town believed it, or pretended to.

But the sheriff had stood on that bank. Had looked into the water. Had known it was a lie.

Now William Ayers was dead. Shot in his bed. Dragged from his sheets like something had pulled him.

And Clara's name carved in his sill?

That was no coincidence.

Farnsworth sat back in the chair, the springs groaning under him. A knock came at the door.

"Come in," he said, already knowing who it was.

The door creaked open. Deputy Stevens, taller now, sterner. A man in his own right, but still learning how to carry the weight of quiet truths.

"There's someone asking questions in town," Stevens said. "A woman. Said her name's Ayers."

"I know," Farnsworth replied.

"She went to see Fields."

"Good."

A pause. Stevens stepped inside, closing the door behind him.

“You think it’s starting again?”

Farnsworth looked down at the map, at the symbol Clara had drawn in charcoal, still faint but clear.

“I think it never stopped,” he said.

He folded the map, slipped the badge into his pocket, and stood.

“I’m going to the Ayers place,” he said. “Before the wrong people get there first.”

Outside, snow clouds gathered above the ridgeline.

The kind that didn't just fall.

The kind that settled.

Chapter 22 – The House at the Edge of the Woods

October 17, 1898 — Ayers Farm, Southeast of Blowville

The farmhouse looked smaller than she remembered.

Perched on a rise just above the bend of the First Fork, it stood like a tired man in the wind; its porch bowed, windows clouded with dust, the wood siding bleached gray by years of rain and silence. The barn had partially collapsed at one corner, and the fence that once corralled goats now leaned like it had given up waiting for repairs.

Rebecca Ayers climbed the porch steps slowly, her boots knocking softly on the hollow boards.

She paused before opening the door.

The lock was broken, the frame splintered near the latch. She stepped inside.

The air was still. Thick with the scent of old paper, damp wood, and a sharp tang she recognized from her time in hospitals; iron and mildew, the ghosts of blood and water.

Her uncle's hat still hung on the hook by the door. A half-carved pipe sat on the table beside his chair. The stove had been cold for days.

She didn't call out. She knew what she'd find: nothing. Whatever had happened here had passed through clean and left the mess behind.

She moved slowly through the kitchen and into the hallway.

The floorboards creaked beneath her weight.

Upstairs, the bedroom door stood open.

The sheriff's men had removed the body, but not the blood. The mattress had been dragged to the floor, where dark stains spread across the pine planks like a wound. The curtains were drawn back, and beyond the frost-etched window, she could see the woods pressing in.

Rebecca turned slowly in place.

That was when she saw it: the carving.

She crossed to the far window, the one that faced west, toward the Freck, and ran her fingers along the sill. There, faint beneath the grain, a name:

C. Moran

The same one Elmer had shown her on the salvaged wood.

But this wasn't a scrap. This was carved here, in this room. By hand.

And beside the name, just barely visible: a mark.

Not a signature. Not initials.

A symbol.

A circle. Four lines. Intersecting like compass points.

She stepped back. Her breath caught.

Something creaked downstairs.

Rebecca froze.

It wasn't wind. Not floor settling.

A step.

She turned slowly and reached for the small iron poker resting near the hearth.

The hallway below remained dark.

Then; movement.

A figure stepped into view at the base of the stairs. Broad-shouldered. Wearing a long coat, hat pulled low. Snow dusted the brim.

He looked up at her with pale eyes.

“Miss Ayers?” came a voice. Calm. Graveled. Familiar.

She exhaled slowly, the poker still clenched in her hand.

Sheriff Farnsworth.

“I thought you might come alone,” he said. “You shouldn’t have.”

She didn’t lower the poker. “You knew I would.”

The old man nodded once.

“I did,” he said. “That’s why I brought this.”

He reached into his coat and held up something wrapped in oilskin.

A small, leather-bound notebook.

Weathered. Torn. Smudged with ash.

Rebecca stepped down the stairs slowly, the poker still in her grip.

“What is that?” she asked.

Farnsworth unwrapped it and handed it to her.

Property of Clara Moran

“This is her last journal,” he said. “The one she carried into the woods.”

Rebecca took it. Opened it.

The first page was dated November 1895.

The second page read:

"If they kill me, it won't be the end. Because the woods remember. And so do I."

* * *

Rebecca sat in the high-backed chair beside the cold stove, the journal resting open across her knees.

Outside, the woods were still. The kind of still that made you check over your shoulder for no good reason.

Sheriff Farnsworth stood near the window, watching the dark fall like a slow curtain.

He hadn't spoken since handing her the book.

She turned the next page.

November 8, 1895 - There are things in this town that don't rot. They linger. Beneath the bark. Behind the boards. Inside the people who forget too easily and those who remember too much.

Fee has eyes everywhere. But he can't see into the woods. Not truly. He fears them like a man fears a locked door he once nailed shut with his own hands. Jonas thinks we're being watched. I think we always were.

Rebecca glanced up. Farnsworth still hadn't moved.

She turned another page.

A sketch, the hollow tree, just as Elmer had described it. Split down the middle. Roots exposed. The clearing around it drawn in charcoal smudges like smoke.

In the margins, Clara had written:

We found something buried. Not bones. Not tools. Something older than both. It was wrapped in symbols. Sealed. But not dead.

I think the land remembers. I think it's starting again.

Rebecca looked to Farnsworth.

"You knew this was real."

"I knew what I saw," he said. "And I knew what would happen if I said it out loud."

She flipped forward, deeper into the journal.

Jonas says the badge belonged to the constable who vanished in 1886. The town said he ran. I think he didn't run far. I think he's still under the hollow, waiting.

They'll kill us for this. They've already tried. But if this book survives, maybe the truth does too.

Maybe someday someone will pick it up and finally ask the right question.

Maybe they'll be braver than I was.

Rebecca felt the words like a hand on her shoulder.

She closed the book slowly and looked up at the sheriff.

"My uncle had this house for thirty years. Why would Clara Moran's name be carved into his windowsill?"

Farnsworth exhaled, finally stepping away from the window.

"Because he saw something, once. Maybe five years ago. Maybe before. Maybe he never told a soul. But some men can't forget what they see, even when they try."

Rebecca stood, holding the journal tight in one hand.

"And now he's dead."

Farnsworth nodded.

"And now it's your turn to decide what you'll do with what he left behind."

Outside, the wind shifted, rising through the trees with a low sigh, like breath held too long finally being let go.

Rebecca crossed to the window and looked into the woods.

Somewhere beyond the river, the hollow tree still stood, its roots gripping something the land wasn't ready to release.

She didn't say it aloud, but she knew.

It had begun again.

Chapter 23 – The Weight of Roots

October 18, 1898 — Fee Brothers Mill House, Above Blowville

Terrence Fee watched the mill through a pane of glass mottled with frost and smoke.

Below, the vats steamed and hissed. Men moved bark on sledges, cursing the cold and the endless tangle of work that no longer paid what it used to. But none of that concerned Fee anymore. The tannery, the lumber contracts, even the title on the Freck, he let others sign now. Younger men. Hungrier men.

He had other things to tend.

Behind him, the fire burned low in the grate. A single candle flickered beside a map laid out on the desk. Not a modern map, not the one used by the county engineers or the tax men. This one was older, hand-drawn. Ink faded. Fibers warped by years and handling.

At the center of it: a circle.

Crossed lines. Compass points. The mark.

The seal.

Fee traced a finger over the ink.

"They never stop coming," he muttered. "Every three years. Like something's keeping the clock."

A knock sounded at the door. Not a servant's knock.

He didn't turn.

"Come in, Crane."

Crane entered, as gaunt as ever, a little more gray in the beard, but the same weight in his eyes. He removed his hat but didn't approach.

Fee asked, “Is it true?”

Crane nodded. “She came to town yesterday. Rebecca Ayers. Met with Fields. Sheriff gave her the journal.”

Fee said nothing.

“She’s staying at the old house. Asked questions at the post. Said she might go south.”

Still nothing.

Then: “Has anyone seen her near the Freck?”

“Not yet.”

Fee turned slowly. His coat was heavy with lined leather, the same one he’d worn the night Jonas and Clara vanished.

“I want her watched. Not followed. Watched. Quietly.”

Crane nodded.

Fee reached into a drawer and retrieved a rusted knife, old, pitted, but still sharp.

“They always dig,” he said, “when they find the edge of something. It’s human nature.”

He held the knife up to the firelight, inspecting the blade.

“But they forget,” he continued, “some things are buried for a reason. And some roots go so deep, you bleed the whole hillside trying to cut them out.”

Crane cleared his throat.

“There’s another thing.”

Fee’s brow lifted.

“The Ayers girl, she asked about the tree.”

The fire cracked.

Fee set the knife down gently and turned back to the window.

“Then she’s already too close.”

He folded the map, slid it into the fire, and watched the edges curl and blacken.

“I want her gone,” he said.

Crane didn’t move.

“Not tonight,” Fee added. “Not sloppy. Not like before. Make it look like grief. Like she saw too much. Like she couldn’t carry what her uncle left behind.”

Crane nodded once and left without a word.

Fee stood alone, watching the last of the map burn.

Outside, the wind stirred the trees.

The same wind from three years ago.

The same silence.

And he knew, the woods would not keep their secret much longer.

Chapter 24 – The Measure of Wood

October 19, 1898 — Blowville

Elmer Fields lit his shop stove with hands that moved slower than they used to, but no less precise.

The mornings had grown colder this week. Not just in temperature, but in tone. There was something in the air again, something tight, like bark ready to peel. He felt it in the way the men spoke at the cookhouse. In the way Sheriff Farnsworth avoided eye contact. In the sound of crows circling the slope above the tannery.

He felt it most when Rebecca Ayers walked into town.

Elmer had seen grief before. But she didn't move like someone grieving. She moved like someone looking, and knowing there was something worth finding.

That scared him more than anything.

He set the coffee pot on the stove and walked to the back of the shop, past the planes and saws, to the cabinet no one touched. He opened it with a key worn smooth over years of hesitation.

Inside were the relics.

A folded map, hand-drawn by Jonas Webber, annotated by Clara Moran.

A metal badge, bent, pitted, stamped with:

PC Constable – 1886

And beneath them both, wrapped in oiled canvas, Clara's original journal, the full version, not the fragments sent out, not the copy Farnsworth gave Rebecca.

He'd kept it hidden.

Not out of fear, but out of purpose. He had always known the time would come again. The Freck did not forgive curiosity. And Fee did not forgive trespass.

He unwrapped the journal and flipped to the last entry:

"We are not buried yet. Not truly. If someone finds this, they must finish what we started. But not by force. By light. By memory. By refusing to forget."

He closed the book.

A knock at the back door.

Soft. Measured.

He opened it to find Farnsworth, coat buttoned high, hat in his hands, eyes red with too little sleep.

"She has the journal," the sheriff said.

"I know," Elmer replied.

"She's going to the tree."

Elmer didn't flinch. "Alone?"

Farnsworth shook his head. "Not if we can help it."

They stepped inside, silent for a moment.

"You think Fee will try again?" Elmer asked.

"He's already moving," the sheriff replied. "Crane's been seen near the Ayers place at night. And someone tried to bribe the post clerk this morning."

Elmer poured two cups of coffee and handed one to Farnsworth.

"So we're back where we started," he said.

"No," the sheriff replied, staring into the cup. "We're where we should have been three years ago. Telling the truth before someone else is buried for it."

Elmer set his cup down.

"I've got the rest of Clara's notes," he said. "We give them to Rebecca. She decides what to do. Not us."

"You trust her that much?"

Elmer looked out the window toward the Freck.

"I trust the kind of person who reads the last page of someone else's life and keeps turning."

Outside, the wind shifted.

And far off in the hills, just past where the last hemlock line broke, a tree cracked.

Not from the cold.

Not from the wind.

From pressure.

* * *

Terrence Fee ran his finger along the edge of the windowpane until the glass fogged beneath his breath.

Below, the tannery fires burned, but they didn't warm him anymore. They hadn't for years. Not since the first time he heard the scream in the clearing, not since the first shovelful of dirt hit the lid of a box that was never supposed to be found.

He turned from the window and walked to the ledger table. It was bare now, save for a single slip of paper and a sealed envelope. On the paper, only two names were written.

R. Ayers
E. Fields

He tapped his finger twice on the page.

Crane stood nearby, gloved hands folded, eyes lowered, not out of respect, but habit.

“Rebecca leaves town tomorrow,” Fee said. “She’ll have that journal in her satchel. Maybe even Clara’s notes.”

Crane didn’t speak.

“I want them recovered. The girl doesn’t matter. But the papers... they do.”

Crane shifted. “She’s asking questions.”

Fee nodded. “Let her. Curiosity is useful. It tells you where to dig.”

He turned to the mantel and picked up a folded slip of survey paper, old and brittle.

“I made a mistake with Clara,” Fee said. “Thought drowning her was enough. Thought silence would settle. But rot always rises, doesn’t it?”

Crane looked up. “What’s the plan?”

Fee slid the envelope across the table.

“You’ll go to the abandoned staging cabin along the trail to the Freck. Take two men. Intercept her before she reaches the clearing.”

“And if she’s not alone?”

Fee didn’t hesitate. “Then they go into the river. Like the others.”

Crane picked up the envelope and nodded once.

Fee turned back to the window.

“It’s the land that’s the problem,” he said softly. “It remembers. And it leaves too many witnesses behind.”

He pressed his palm flat to the cold glass.

“Sooner or later,” he whispered, “the rest of the tree comes down. Or everything else does.”

Chapter 25 – Into the Clearing

October 20, 1898 — The Freck Warrant

The trail to the Freck hadn't seen real footsteps in years.

Rebecca's boots cracked through thin crusts of frost as she climbed the rise beyond Blowville, following the path marked faintly in Clara's journal. It wasn't a proper trail, just a series of notations: "cut left at the old gate," "pass where the pines narrow," "look for the ash stump with three iron nails."

She carried a satchel across her chest. Inside it, wrapped in wool, were Clara's words, Elmer's map, and a folded page of her own, a single line scrawled with ink the night before:

If they bury me, it won't be deep enough.

The woods were quiet. Not the soft hush of falling leaves or wind in branches, but the kind of stillness that waited.

She paused near a half-rotted log and checked her bearings. Ahead, the slope curled down into a hollow, its floor blanketed with old needles and the remains of last spring's runoff.

At the bottom of that hollow stood the tree.

She didn't need Clara's drawing to recognize it. The split hemlock, gnarled and blackened, its trunk cracked like a yawning mouth, roots curling up like the knuckles of a buried hand.

Rebecca stepped into the clearing.

The air changed.

Cooler. Still.

The sound of the wind vanished, as if swallowed.

She moved slowly around the base of the tree, tracing the

same symbols etched faintly into the bark, the circle and lines, weathered but still visible.

She knelt and brushed aside moss and leaves.

There, beneath the roots, stone.

A seam. A door. Maybe just the memory of one.

She reached for the journal, flipped through to Clara's sketch of the entrance. The drawing matched what lay before her. Down to the way one root curled across the stone like a lock.

She reached for her small hand-trowel.

Then; a branch snapped.

She froze.

Not behind her.

Above.

She looked up in time to see the flicker of a coat through the trees, dark wool, low hat, too still for a hunter.

Her breath caught.

Crane.

She didn't know the name, but the shape was unmistakable, the way the shoulders hunched, the way the eyes followed without blinking.

He wasn't alone.

Two more men moved through the undergrowth, flanking the clearing like dogs circling a foxhole.

Rebecca backed toward the base of the tree.

They hadn't seen her yet.

She slid the satchel behind the twisted root and stood.

If they were going to kill her, they'd get words first.

The man in the middle, Crane, stepped into the clearing.

His eyes met hers.

Rebecca didn't flinch.

"You're not supposed to be here," he said, calm as water.

She stared back. "Then you remember what happened to the last woman who was."

He smiled, just barely. "We made it look like an accident."

"I don't do accidents," she said.

Behind her, the wind picked up. But only in the trees. Not in the clearing.

The air around the hollow tree remained still.

Almost...watchful.

Crane raised a hand. The other men stepped forward.

Rebecca's fingers tightened around the trowel.

She took one step back. Then; a shotgun cracked.

Crane staggered.

Rebecca dropped flat to the ground.

Voices shouted. Another shot rang out, closer this time.

And from the ridgeline, moving fast through the brush, came Elmer Fields and Sheriff Farnsworth, rifles drawn, eyes hard.

The men scattered, Crane slipping back into the trees with one hand bleeding.

Farnsworth knelt beside Rebecca.

"Thought you might come alone," he said, panting.

She looked at him. "You were right."

Behind them, the wind finally entered the clearing.

And somewhere deep beneath the roots, the ground seemed to sigh.

* * *

The knock at the door wasn't soft. It was soaked in blood.

Fee stood by the hearth, poker in hand, staring at the fire when Crane stumbled through the frame.

He was pale, teeth clenched, his left arm wrapped in a butchered bandage, blood blooming through the cloth like a rose. His coat was shredded. His breath came in grunts.

Behind him, one of the other men, a boy, barely twenty, carried a pack that wasn't his and wore the expression of someone who'd seen the end of something.

"She had company," Crane hissed.

Fee didn't move. "How many?"

"Two," the boy said. "Sheriff. Fields. Came in from the ridge. Knew where we were. They were waiting."

Fee stepped forward, slow.

He looked at Crane's hand, or what was left of it.

"You lost it?"

Crane nodded once. "Buckshot. Took the whole palm. Can't feel the fingers."

Fee turned to the fireplace and fed in another log. The flames hissed.

"No journal?" he asked.

"No," the boy said quickly. "She dropped it behind the tree. We couldn't get to it."

Fee said nothing for a long time.

Then he walked to the sideboard, opened a narrow drawer, and pulled out a small brass case. Inside, a razor-sharp skinning knife, never used.

He held it up in the firelight. The boy took a step back. Crane didn't.

Fee set the knife down.

"This isn't about a girl anymore," he said, voice low. "This is about the town. About the mill. About what we built from bark and silence."

Crane sat down heavily in the chair by the hearth, his breath sharp through his teeth.

"She saw it," he muttered. "The seal. The clearing. Same place as before."

Fee stared into the fire, his eyes twin embers. "She saw too much."

A long silence passed between them.

The boy dared to speak again. "What do we do now?"

Fee turned to face him.

"Now," he said, "we finish it. Not with blades. Not with bullets. But with fire."

He stepped toward the map cabinet and pulled out a rolled parchment, the last original plot of the Freck warrant, with the clearing marked in black ink.

“We burn the tree,” he said. “We collapse the roots. We salt the ground.”

The boy looked uncertain. “What if someone saw? What if they tell the papers?”

Fee looked at Crane.

Crane met his eyes, grim and white-faced. “Then we burn the story, too.”

Chapter 26 – Beneath the Hemlock

October 20, 1898 (dusk) — The Freck Warrant

The clearing was darker now.

The sun had gone behind the ridge, and the cold came quickly with it, settling like breath held too long. The hemlock's roots reached across the forest floor, black fingers tangled in stone. At the center, the tree yawned open, silent, wounded, waiting.

Rebecca sat near the base, hands still shaking. The satchel was clutched tight to her chest, blood from Crane's wound still spattered on the outer flap.

Across from her, Sheriff Farnsworth reloaded his shotgun by the light of a lantern. Elmer Fields crouched near the exposed seam of earth and root, clearing moss from the stone ring they'd uncovered.

They were alive. But that wasn't victory, not here. Not yet.

"What do we do now?" Rebecca asked quietly.

Farnsworth didn't look up. "Fee won't stop."

"No," Elmer said, brushing away another layer of dirt. "He's coming. Likely tonight."

He reached beneath a curled root and pulled free a flat, square stone, worn smooth, carved at the edges. Beneath it, darkness opened. A narrow passage. Cool air rose from the earth. It smelled like wet iron and old things.

Rebecca stepped forward.

"This is the place, isn't it?"

Elmer nodded. "A door, of sorts. Or a mouth. Depends on how you look at it."

They lowered the lantern into the hollow.

The light barely touched the bottom, just a flicker of stone wall, something metal glinting faintly in the dark.

"I never went in," Elmer admitted. "Not even when Clara first found it."

Farnsworth said nothing.

Rebecca looked at both men. "You're not going to stop me, are you?"

"No," the sheriff replied. "We're going to go with you."

They didn't speak as they tied the ropes.

One by one, they descended, Elmer first, then Rebecca, then Farnsworth, into the earth beneath the tree. The shaft was tight, maybe seven feet down, opening into a space no wider than a logging bunkhouse. Walls of fitted stone. Timber supports blackened with age.

At the center, a crate. Not large. Not marked. Wrapped in chain.

Beside it, a rusted shovel and a strip of bark with something burned into it:

BELOW

Rebecca ran her fingers along the wood. It was damp. Still pliable. The symbol was carved beneath the word, circle, crossed lines.

Elmer stared at the crate.

"It's not locked," he said.

Farnsworth raised the lantern.

And in that moment, something above them shifted.

A groan. A low vibration. Then: smoke.

It curled down the shaft like a snake.

Farnsworth moved fast.

"Out. Now."

Rebecca scrambled to the rope. Elmer pushed her up.

Farnsworth handed her the journal and the satchel before climbing.

The smoke thickened, not from the fire, not yet. This smoke was greasy, chemical. Not woodsmoke, but accelerant.

They reached the surface as flame caught the edge of the clearing. Fee's fire, lit at the perimeter, crawling inward with purpose.

Farnsworth grabbed Rebecca's hand.

"Run."

They ran.

Behind them, the clearing glowed. The hollow tree, once quiet and ancient, began to scream, not with sound, but with heat and cracking wood.

And in the cellar below, the crate remained untouched.

But something inside it stirred.

* * *

Terrence Fee stood beneath a stand of white pine, his breath rising in ribbons as the fire licked up from the clearing.

The men he'd brought stayed back on the slope, watching with unease. Even Crane, his arm now bound in rough canvas and reeking of whiskey and pine tar, kept his distance. The pain had turned his jaw slack and his eyes wild, but it was nothing compared to the look in Fee's.

The blaze moved fast. Not because the woods were dry, but because Fee had planned it that way.

Oil and pitch, tucked beneath the moss months ago. Quietly. Carefully. For this.

The hollow tree was a pyre now, flames pouring from its split trunk like breath from a throat too long sealed. Sparks danced into the sky. The bark peeled back with sharp cracks.

Fee didn't blink.

"You hear that?" he asked.

No one answered.

"They say the trees scream when they fall," he said, his voice low. "But it's not the trees. It's the roots."

He stepped forward, closer to the heat.

"Everything below starts to tear. And the ground remembers what's been buried there."

Behind him, Crane muttered, "You think it's enough?"

Fee stared into the blaze.

"I know it is."

But even as he said it, he felt the air shift.

Something in the way the flames leaned, as if blown from within. A sudden drop in pressure, like the hollow tree had exhaled for the first time in years.

The clearing began to collapse inward. Not dramatically. Just subtly. A slow settling, as if the earth itself was tired of holding the secret in place.

Fee's heart slowed. Not with calm. With the kind of fear that came too late.

He turned from the fire, teeth clenched.

“Tell the men we leave now,” he snapped.

“But…”

“Now.”

As they moved back down the slope, smoke trailing behind them, Fee paused for one last glance over his shoulder.

The tree was gone. Ash now. But not silence.

The fire still burned. But the quiet beneath it had changed.

Whatever was buried wasn’t buried anymore.

Chapter 27 – Ash Between the Pines

October 20, 1898 (near midnight) — Northern Edge of the Freck Warrant

They crouched beneath a crown of spruce and pine, their breath ragged in the freezing dark. Smoke rolled uphill from the clearing behind them, dragging firelight through the trees like the last flicker of a dying eye.

The hollow tree was gone. Burned to ash. Its roots collapsed inward like a mouth sealed in death.

But what it had covered, that low chamber, the crated shape beneath the earth, remained.

Rebecca sat with her back against a fallen log, her gloved hand wrapped tightly around the satchel in her lap. The journal pressed against her ribs like a second heartbeat.

She could still see the crate in her mind, chained, heavy, old. Something her uncle might have seen. Might have touched.

That was the part she couldn't shake.

"What did my uncle know about this place?" she asked aloud, voice low. "What was he doing out here three years ago?"

Elmer Fields looked over, his face drawn in the red flicker of dying fire.

"He never said a word to anyone," he replied. "Not to me. Not to Farnsworth. But he kept to himself more after '95. Started building fences where there was no livestock. Locked the root cellar with three bolts."

Farnsworth didn't speak. He was perched just ahead of them, watching the slope for movement.

"Do you think he helped Clara?" Rebecca asked. "Back then?"

Elmer exhaled slowly. "He may have tried. But that kind of help… it sticks to a man."

"You think that's why they killed him?"

Farnsworth turned. "I think William Ayers saw something he wasn't supposed to. And I think someone decided he couldn't die quiet."

A branch cracked somewhere below.

They froze.

Lanterns bobbed in the woods near the clearing. Three shapes, two with rifles, one with a torch, walked a loose spiral around the burned clearing, their boots kicking through ash and broken root.

They weren't searching yet. Not actively. But it was only a matter of time.

Rebecca crouched lower, the journal held tight beneath her coat.

"I think he was trying to leave me a trail," she whispered. "The carving. Clara's name. The symbol. He didn't just remember, he wanted someone to ask."

Elmer nodded. "And now you're asking."

"And they're trying to stop me for it."

Farnsworth glanced toward the firelight. "They'll be back at first light. Wide sweep. Tree line to river."

"Then we leave before dawn," Rebecca said. "Take the long way north."

"Not by the Pike," Elmer added. "They'll have riders. Too many eyes."

Farnsworth adjusted his shotgun. "We take the river. South.

Quiet and cold. If your uncle could've done it over, maybe that's what he'd have done."

Rebecca stared back toward the glow rising from the clearing.

"And what if he buried something?" she asked. "Something deeper than the crate. Something they didn't find?"

No one answered. Because they were all thinking the same thing.

If William Ayers had tried to warn her, he'd done it with marks and silence, the only language Blowville allowed its dead.

She pressed the satchel closer.

"Then we carry it," she said. "All of it. Until we find someone who'll listen."

The fire flared once more, then dimmed into coals.

And beneath the forest floor, where roots no longer held the shape of the tree, something long-buried stirred against the chain.

Chapter 28 – Smoke Over Town

October 21, 1898 — Blowville

By morning, the smoke had rolled all the way into town.

It drifted above the rooftops of Main Street, hung low between the mill stacks and the frame of the boarding house. The townspeople stepped out onto porches with handkerchiefs over their faces and eyes already narrowed. They knew what fire meant. They'd seen enough of it in the tannery pits, the dry yards, the boiler sheds.

But this was different.

This wasn't accident or industry.

This was the Freck.

By noon, two rumors were already circling the cookhouse:

1. The old tree line had caught from another lightning strike

2. Rebecca Ayers had gone missing, just like her uncle, just like Clara Moran.

Neither version made sense.

At the general store, Mrs. Boyle said she'd seen Fee's man Crane ride out the night before with two others, bundled in pitch-soaked cloaks.

At the mill, bark men talked in low voices. About Clara. About Jonas. About how silence always seemed to follow anyone who got too close to the Freck.

At the pig's ear, the regulars raised their glasses when William Ayers's name came up. But they didn't toast. They just drank.

"Good man," someone muttered. "Kept to himself."

“Good man,” someone else echoed, “but wrong friends.”

Only one voice, Ira Shelburn, the postmaster, spoke loud enough to hear:

“She came looking for answers,” he said, wiping his glasses, “and now the answers are ash.”

No one replied.

Because in Blowville, words were flint.

And Fee had the matches.

* * *

Near the tannery, Terrence Fee walked the yard with a calm expression, nodding to workers, inspecting the boilers, reviewing rail shipments. But behind his eyes, there was fire.

He knew the story was already slipping. He’d fed it to the town through careful hands; Crane whispering to the postmaster, a few well-timed “witnesses” who saw lightning and nothing else.

But doubt was an ember. And once it lit, it traveled.

He returned to his office that afternoon and stared out over the rooftops.

From here, you couldn’t see the tree line anymore. Just the smoke.

Still rising. Still watching.

He turned back to his desk and took out a clean sheet of paper.

To: Mr. Hale – State Forestry Bureau, Williamsport
Subject: Proposed Sale – Freck Tract, Full Transfer

Fee dipped his pen and began to write.

Because if the land kept secrets, the best way to keep it silent…

…was to sell it to someone who didn’t ask questions.

Chapter 29 – Down the First Fork

October 21, 1898 (before dawn) — South of Blowville

The river was barely moving.

Mist hung above the First Fork in soft coils, ghosting along the surface as if the woods themselves were exhaling after the fire. Rebecca Ayers sat in the center of the narrow skiff, knees pulled tight to her chest, clutching the satchel that now held more than just Clara's journal, it held a promise.

Behind her, Elmer Fields guided the stern, one oar dipping quietly, methodically, keeping them to the slow current. Sheriff Farnsworth sat in the bow, shotgun across his lap, eyes on the banks as the dark hills of the Freck slid silently past.

They had left the ridge before first light, when the ashes still glowed red behind them and Fee's riders were just shadows whispering through the trees. The fire hadn't been enough. They knew that now. Whatever secrets had been hidden beneath the hollow tree were not gone.

Only loosened.

Rebecca had barely spoken since they launched. She could feel it, that sensation she couldn't explain, like her uncle's voice was somewhere nearby. Like the weight of the truth wasn't just ink and parchment but something that watched, something that had followed them into the water.

Elmer finally broke the silence. "We'll hit Sinnamahoning by sundown if the current holds."

"Assuming no one's waiting," Farnsworth added.

Rebecca looked at them both. "You think Fee sent riders?"

Farnsworth didn't answer. He didn't have to.

Fee wasn't the kind of man who left a fire burning without watching what crawled out of it.

They passed a bend in the river where a pair of fox tracks crossed the muddy bank. An old hunting camp sat slumped under a leaning birch, its tin chimney bent like a broken finger. The kind of place her uncle might have known. Might have used.

Rebecca leaned forward.

“William knew about the tree,” she said, softly. “He must’ve been there. Maybe he helped Clara bury the crate. Maybe he even locked it himself.”

Elmer’s jaw tensed. “If he did, he died trying to keep it closed.”

“And I think Fee killed him for it,” she said.

Farnsworth gave a slow nod. “Not with a rope or a rifle. With doubt. With a whisper no one questions.”

Rebecca opened the satchel and pulled out Clara’s journal. She flipped to the last page, the one written in haste, almost illegible.

If they kill me, find the tree. If they burn it, find what’s left. If they chase you, run faster than I did.

She closed the book.

“I won’t stop,” she said. “Even if they follow us to Sinnamahoning. Even if they follow us to Harrisburg.”

“We know,” Elmer said.

Farnsworth shifted the shotgun.

“That’s why we’re still here.”

* * *

The current pulled them around another bend, and for a moment the trees broke, revealing the long slope of forested valley between the Freck and the First Fork. Smoke still curled above the treetops in the distance, but it was fading now.

In its place, wind returned.

And beneath it, the river kept speaking, moving slow and steady, like it carried memory between its banks.

They were no longer running from Blowville.

They were bringing it with them.

By the time they reached the narrow dock outside Sinnamahoning, the sun had dropped behind the western ridge, and the water had gone still as glass.

The First Fork let them go without sound.

Rebecca stepped off the skiff with aching knees, her boots slipping slightly on the damp planks. Her satchel was still slung across her shoulder, the strap worn from where she'd clutched it too tightly. It felt heavier now, like the pages inside had gained weight with every mile.

The town lay just up the bank, small, quiet, tucked into the bend like it didn't want to be seen. A general store. A post office. A few houses with lamps glowing warm behind frosted windows. A rail spur cut across the edge of town, the tracks silent, the depot shuttered.

Elmer tied off the skiff while Farnsworth scanned the shoreline.

"I used to come here for lumber contracts," Elmer said. "Ten years back. Town hasn't changed."

"Think anyone'll help us?" Rebecca asked.

Farnsworth gave her a sidelong look. "Depends how many friends Fee has this far south."

They made for the post office first, crossing the muddy

street with their collars turned up. Inside, a bell above the door chimed faintly, and a man behind the counter, older, with wire spectacles and an ink-stained shirt, looked up from a ledger.

"We need to send something," Rebecca said before he could speak. "Two packets. One to Harrisburg. One to Baltimore. Personal delivery if you have it."

The man raised an eyebrow. "Payment?"

Farnsworth stepped forward and set a silver watch on the counter.

"Family piece," he said. "Worth enough."

The clerk looked at them, three strangers, soot-stained and travel-worn, and saw more than he let on. He took the watch.

"I'll see it done," he said.

Outside, the street had grown darker. A storm gathered somewhere past the ridgeline. The first cold drops began to fall.

Rebecca exhaled.

The packets were gone.

Clara's words. Jonas's maps. Elmer's recollection. Her uncle's silence. All of it, riding iron rails into the world.

Now they waited.

They found a small room above the depot, one of the old bunks kept for passing rail workers. The woman who gave them the key didn't ask names. Just handed them a blanket and shut the door behind her.

Inside, the three of them sat on crates around a potbelly stove that barely held a coal.

“It’s out now,” Elmer said quietly. “What we carried.”

“And what we left behind,” Rebecca added.

Farnsworth leaned back, boots crossed. “If Fee wants to keep it buried, he’ll have to kill the country to do it.”

The wind rose beyond the glass, and a freight engine moaned somewhere far off in the valley.

Rebecca didn’t sleep that night.

She watched the shadows in the corner of the room and listened for footsteps that never came.

But she kept Clara’s journal open in her lap.

And in the margin, where Clara had once written:

If they bury me, it won’t be deep enough...

Rebecca added, in her own hand:

You were right.

* * *

Fee stood at the edge of the mill yard, coat flapping in the rising wind, watching smoke still rise from the black line of forest.

The fire had done its work, but it hadn’t been enough.

The hollow tree was gone. The clearing had collapsed. But three had made it out.

He turned as Crane limped up the path from the stables, a fresh bandage wrapped around the stump where his hand used to be. His face was bloodless, jaw clenched from the morphine.

“Got word from the Pike,” Crane rasped. “Clerk at

Sinnamahoning recognized Fields. Girl was with him. Sheriff too."

Fee said nothing.

"They sent letters," Crane added. "One to Harrisburg. One to Baltimore."

Fee turned back toward the woods, silent.

Crane tried to sound casual. "I can go after them. Take the northern spur. They'll hole up in town, maybe a day or two…"

"No," Fee said.

Crane stopped. "Then what?"

Fee finally faced him. His eyes were colder than the wind.

"If we chase them now, we look like criminals. If we wait, we look like men."

Crane frowned. "They've already spoken."

"Then we speak louder."

Fee walked across the yard toward the company office, boots cracking through frost.

Inside, he sat at the broad desk and opened a drawer.

Out came a ledger, the one marked with names, debts, and favors. He flipped to a page near the back, where the handwriting turned more careful. Political names. Men with ink on their hands and clean boots that had never touched mud.

He pulled out three envelopes. One was already addressed:

Mr. Alvin Thresher – State Police Bureau, Harrisburg

He dipped his pen in ink and began writing.

Rebecca Ayers would be labeled an arsonist. Sheriff Farnsworth, a drunk and a deserter. Elmer Fields, an unregistered veteran with illegal arms and a history of trespass.

By morning, the telegraphs would hum. The law would move, not to protect, but to erase.

Because Fee didn't need to chase them.

He only needed the world to stop listening.

As the wind howled down from the Freck and rattled the shutters, he pressed the seal on the last envelope.

He whispered to the empty office, as if the land itself could still hear:

"You should've stayed buried."

Chapter 30 – More Ink and More Ash

October 22–23, 1898 — Potter County, Harrisburg, and Beyond

The first newspaper article ran the next day.

Not in Blowville. Not even in Sinnamahoning.

But in Coudersport, slipped into the second column of the *Potter Enterprise* between a report on railroad delays and an obituary for a former mill superintendent.

Strange Blaze North of Blowville — Local Sheriff Abandons Post

Sources say Horace Farnsworth, former sheriff of Blowville, is under investigation for dereliction of duty after disappearing from his office two nights ago. The timing coincides with a suspicious blaze in the remote Freck warrant, where illegal surveying and possible arson are being investigated by company officials.

Two paragraphs later:

Farnsworth was reportedly seen with Elmer Fields, a former carpenter known to have disputes with Fee Brothers management, and a young woman claiming to be the niece of William Ayers, a reclusive farmer recently found dead under unusual circumstances.

The word *unusual* did a lot of work.

So did *claiming*.

And just like that, Rebecca Ayers was not a witness.

She was a stranger, an outsider, a questionable relative with a curious interest in company land.

By nightfall, the wires lit up with telegrams, quiet, indirect, shaped to avoid legal liability.

In Williamsport, a clerk in the Forestry Bureau received a note about trespassers in the Freck.

In Harrisburg, a state constable was instructed to "verify the sudden activity" of a former sheriff with a record of "non-cooperation."

In Baltimore, a letter was intercepted and re-routed, its contents read, logged, and sealed.

Fee didn't need to prove anything. He only needed to muddy it.

And Blowville, what it was, what it remembered, stayed silent.

The old men at the mill called Farnsworth a coward.

The bark-yard laborers whispered that Elmer had been caught stealing timber.

And Rebecca?

She became a story. A widow-in-advance, a girl who had "wandered too far into old business," chasing shadows in trees that had long since been cleared.

No mention of the crate. No mention of Clara. No mention of what had burned in the clearing.

Just smoke.

Just silence.

Just the kind of forgetting that comes with a signature and a newspaper fold.

The copy of the *Potter Enterprise* arrived by train, folded twice and damp at the edges.

Rebecca Ayers read the article while standing beneath the depot awning, the storm clouds rolling low behind her. She didn't speak. Didn't curse. Just read it twice, then once more, until the words blurred, not from rain but from the sharp heat behind her eyes.

Farnsworth stood beside her, his jaw working slowly. Elmer Fields leaned against the post, arms crossed.

“They didn’t just smear us,” Rebecca said quietly. “They rewrote the whole thing.”

“They used my name,” Farnsworth muttered. “And left out hers.” He didn’t have to explain. Clara Moran’s name was gone.

Rebecca folded the paper slowly and slipped it into her satchel beside the journal.

“I expected this,” she said.

“You don’t sound surprised,” Elmer said.

“I’m not. But I am angry.” She turned to both men, her voice steady now, colder.

“They’re trying to erase us the same way they buried Jonas. The same way they tried to bury Clara. The difference is… they didn’t know I’d read every line she left behind.”

Elmer nodded slowly. “And?”

Rebecca pulled out the final pages of the journal, Clara’s last entries, hastily transcribed over two winters, half of them smudged with tears or fire-dust. She laid them across the crate they’d dragged into the depot storeroom.

“We find someone who prints,” she said. “Not lawyers. Not clerks. Typesetters. Newsmen. The kind who still believe that words mean something.”

Farnsworth frowned. “They’ll try to stop that too.”

“They already are,” she said. “But now we know their tools. We use ours.”

She pulled out her notebook, the one she'd begun the morning after the fire, and wrote at the top of the first page:

What They Tried to Burn.

She turned to the two men beside her.

"Clara told the truth. Now I'll tell what they did to her truth."

And for the first time since leaving the Freck, Rebecca smiled.

Not out of joy. But out of conviction.

Fee had fire. But she had testimony. And testimony, once spoken loud enough, once set in print, couldn't be put back in the ground.

Chapter 31 – The Typesetter's Table

October 26, 1898 — Emporium, Pennsylvania

The printing office was warmer than expected.

It sat on the edge of Fourth Street, half-tucked behind a feed store and a blacksmith's stall, its shingle faded from years of soot and rain:

The Cameron County Herald – Weekly Since 1857

Rebecca Ayers stepped inside carrying her satchel, the brass bell above the door jangling like it hadn't been rung in days. The place smelled of ink, old paper, and something charred, familiar now.

A man in his fifties hunched over the composing table, sleeves rolled, spectacles low on his nose. He was sorting slugs for the weekend's broadsheet: wheat prices, a timber notice, and a quote from a county commissioner that no one would remember.

He didn't look up. "If you're selling ad space, I'm full through November."

"I'm not," Rebecca said. "I'm selling the truth."

That made him glance over the rims of his glasses.

He set down a brass type slug and turned toward her fully.

"Name's Henry Blodgett," he said. "Editor, typesetter, janitor. What truth are you selling, Miss?"

She unbuckled the satchel and placed Clara Moran's journal on the table.

Blodgett raised an eyebrow. "That's a name I haven't heard in years."

Rebecca opened to the first entry.

"She was murdered," she said flatly. "They made it look like a drowning. Burned the place where she hid this. Tried to bury the rest of the story under timber rights and company paper."

Blodgett looked at the worn, scorched journal.

He saw more than ink. He saw proof.

She handed him the packet Elmer had helped assemble; maps, sketches, a sworn statement from Farnsworth, and a transcript of William Ayers's will. The last page bore her own signature.

"I'm not asking for charity," she said. "Just space. A column. A serial. A whisper loud enough to reach Harrisburg."

Blodgett didn't touch the papers right away.

But his eyes softened. "You know what happens if I print this?"

"I do."

"They'll threaten you."

"They already have."

He stared at her, this stranger with soot in her coat seams and conviction in her voice.

Then he pulled a sheet of blank galley paper from the drawer and slid it across the table.

"I set in twelve-point Gothic," he said. "Lead with a headline."

Rebecca nodded and wrote:

The Hollow Tree: What They Tried to Burn
A True Account of Murder, Memory, and the Forest That Remembers

Blodgett read it aloud under his breath.

Then he picked up the first page of Clara's journal and ran his fingers along the edge.

"I'll need a day," he said.

Rebecca exhaled and turned toward the door.

"Take two," she replied. "But not three. There's more coming."

As she stepped outside, the setting sun filtered through coal haze, and the wind smelled faintly of hemlock, even here.

The story had left the woods.

Now it was going to print.

* * *

Rebecca stepped out of the printing office onto the cobbled streets of Emporium.

The lamplighters were making their rounds. Horses clopped over cobblestone. A freight engine moaned down the line a mile away. The town was modest, tucked into the folds of the Alleghenies, but it had something Blowville never did: eyes that looked outward.

She crossed to the boarding house across from the depot, where Farnsworth and Elmer had secured a room under false names. The stairs creaked as she climbed them, each step like a clock ticking closer to something she couldn't yet name.

Inside, the men sat at a small table, hunched over a spread of the *Potter Enterprise* and a county map.

Elmer looked up as she entered. "Well?"

"He's printing it," she said. "First edition goes out Friday."

Farnsworth gave a low whistle and folded his arms. "Then we'd better be gone by Friday morning."

"They'll be watching the rail lines," Rebecca said.

"They're already watching us," Elmer added. "Doesn't matter what we do next. Fee knows it's in motion. The only thing left is whether the world listens."

Rebecca walked to the window. She could see the lights of the typesetter's shop down the street, still glowing in the twilight.

"It's not just about listening," she said. "It's about remembering."

She set her satchel down and opened her own notebook.

On the first blank page, she began to write, not as Clara. Not as a witness to someone else's story.

But as herself.

The fire did not end it. The tree fell, but the roots held. They always do.

I am writing because someone has to. Because truth survives in the margins, if someone bothers to read them.

She didn't stop. Not until the wind outside whistled sharp through the cracks in the glass. Not until her hand cramped. Not until her heart, which had been burning since the night they fled the Freck, finally began to slow.

Elmer watched her. "You're not done, are you?"

She shook her head. "No. I'm just getting started."

He smiled. "Then so are we."

The three of them sat in silence as the room dimmed.

And on the desk, between an empty cup and a folding knife, her pen kept moving.

Because what they tried to burn was still alive.

Chapter 32 – What the Roots Held

October 27, 1898 — The Freck Warrant

Smoke still curled above the ridge, but the fire had long since gone cold.

Charred hemlock lay in brittle arcs across the forest floor, its once-ancient trunk now ash and memory. Around the hollow, the moss had blackened. The air smelled like boiled iron and wet stone, though no rain had fallen.

There were no men now.

No voices.

Just a silence so deep it seemed to stretch backward in time.

And then, the earth moved.

Only slightly.

A slow, breath-like swell at the center of the clearing, where the roots had collapsed, where the crate had once been buried, chained and sealed in a cellar, beneath the weight of a tree that had grown above it like a scar.

Something shifted beneath the broken floor.

Not with force. Not with violence.

With deliberation.

The stones that once sealed the chamber had cracked in the fire. One had tumbled free. A narrow gap remained, a black wedge where no light entered and yet something within it gleamed.

A line of frost formed along the soil, spidering out in a perfect circle, as if the clearing were being claimed.

Then, from the gap:

a sound.

Not speech. Not breath.

Just a low scrape, metal against stone, or bone against timber. The sound of movement after long stillness. The sound of something remembering its shape.

A raven landed on a scorched branch and immediately took flight again, cawing once, sharp and panicked.

And then:

From beneath the root chamber, something emerged.

Not fast.

Not whole.

A shape that moved without being seen, only felt, like wind without a breeze. It passed through the ashes, brushing against bark and branch and bone. It left no footprint.

Only silence.

And behind it, the circle carved into stone began to glow, faint, pulsing like a heartbeat.

It was out.

And it was moving, slowly, deliberately, toward the town that had tried to forget it.

Toward the stories being told again.

Toward the names it once knew.

Chapter 33 – Hollow Echoes

October 27, 1898 — Blowville

Terrence Fee awoke before dawn with the taste of ash in his mouth.

He sat up in the dark, the blanket falling from his chest like something unclean. The room was still. Too still. Not the quiet of sleep, but the stillness of absence.

For a moment, he didn't know where he was.

Then he saw the faint outline of the mill through the window, the gray slouch of chimneys, the bark piles motionless in the yard.

Home. Control.

He stood, crossed to the washbasin, and splashed water on his face. It was cold, sharper than it should've been for October. His hands trembled slightly.

He hadn't dreamt. He never did. But something had woken him anyway.

Downstairs, the office smelled of boiled ink and damp wool. Crane hadn't returned yet. No new telegraphs. No new fires. Just quiet. Almost as if nothing remained of the tree.

But Fee felt it.

He opened the drawer of his desk and took out the ledger, flipping past names, debts, shipments. Past the survey contracts and the shell companies. Past the men who signed their silence in whiskey and wire.

And he stopped at a page Clara had once touched, he remembered the moment clearly. She'd stood across this very desk, years ago, asking questions about root systems and property lines and why the Freck wasn't logged like the rest.

He had laughed then.

She hadn't.

Fee stared at the page now, and for the first time, he saw something he hadn't before.

A faint smudge in the margin.

A circle. Four faint lines. The seal.

But he'd never marked it. No one had.

He closed the book slowly and looked out the window.

A single bird moved across the sky, jerking, fast, black as coal. Not a crow. Not quite.

It circled once, then vanished behind the ridge.

He turned to the fireplace and reached for the poker.

Not because it was cold.

But because something inside him, something older than instinct, told him he wasn't alone anymore.

Not in this room.

Not in this town.

Not in the land he thought he owned.

* * *

The knock came just after first light.

Fee opened the door himself, sleeves rolled, the fire still cold behind him.

Crane stood in the threshold, soaked from the waist down, his stump newly bandaged and his face pale beneath three days of sweat and travel.

"She made it," Crane said without preamble. "Emporium."

Fee didn't move. "And?"

"She's handed over the journal. The map. Blodgett's press is running the first column tonight."

Fee's throat worked, but he said nothing.

Crane continued. "They've titled it *The Hollow Tree*. They're printing Clara's name. Yours. Mine. The clearing."

He finally held out a sheet of newsprint: torn, smudged from the bottom of a train satchel.

Fee took it. Read the headline.

The Hollow Tree: What They Tried to Burn
by Rebecca Ayers

His jaw tightened, eyes scanning the first lines: Clara's voice brought back to life, speaking plainly of bodies in creeks, of ledgers cooked, of trees carved with symbols no surveyor ever learned in school.

"Do they believe her?" Fee asked.

Crane shifted. "Not yet. But they're listening."

Fee turned slowly and walked back inside.

He sat. The paper still trembled slightly in his hand. He didn't speak for nearly a minute.

Then:

"Set the wire to Harrisburg. We triple the offer to the Forestry Bureau. Tell them the Freck's unstable; burn scar, falling roots, animal hazards. Make it sound like a liability waiting to become their problem."

Crane nodded. "And the press?"

Fee looked up. His eyes were distant, like someone listening to something just out of earshot.

"We wait. Let the story hit. Let them get a taste of it. Then we smear her again, harder. Print Clara's grandfather's debts. Dig up whatever we can on the Ayers family."

"And if it doesn't work?"

Fee stood.

He walked to the ledger and ripped out the page Clara had once touched. The one with the faint seal. He held it over the fireplace and watched it burn.

"If it doesn't work," he said softly, "then we dig up what's left beneath the Freck and make sure no one else wants to go looking."

Crane didn't reply.

And for the first time, Fee didn't look victorious. He looked cornered.

The fire crackled. The woods, silent beyond the window, waited. And in the ridgelines above Blowville, smoke began to rise again, but this time, not from Fee's fire.

Chapter 34 – When the Paper Hits the Floor

October 28, 1898 — Across Pennsylvania

The printing ink was still wet when the first copies of *The Cameron County Herald* hit stoops and counters across Emporium, Driftwood, and Sinnamahoning.

By noon, they'd reached Benezette, Austin, and the edge of Galeton.

By dusk, the headline had made its way to Coudersport.

The Hollow Tree: What They Tried to Burn
A True Account by Rebecca Ayers, With Pages from the Journal of Clara Moran

It was laid out in full column width on the front page, edged with a hand-drawn facsimile of Clara's seal. The piece pulled no punches, naming Fee, describing the fire, the false drownings, the vanished crate, the uncut Freck, and the marks etched into both bark and bone.

At the Emporium post office, the clerk read the first paragraph out loud to a line of waiting customers.

At a boarding house in Driftwood, a traveling sales agent underlined the word "murdered" three times and folded the paper into his valise.

At a lumber camp east of Sinnamahoning, two bark peelers passed the article between them in silence, then walked to the edge of the clearing and stared at the line of untouched forest with new eyes.

Not everyone believed it.

At the Emporium depot, a merchant called it "a girl's fantasy" and waved it off before finishing the article. But he read it again that night, this time with the door locked.

At the Coudersport courthouse, a junior clerk filed the issue between timber claims and property disputes, but circled a passage describing Clara Moran's disappearance.

And in the corner of a general store in Benezette, an old woman tapped the symbol printed in the corner and whispered, "I've seen that before."

* * *

That night, the printing press ran longer than scheduled.

Blodgett reprinted an extra 300 copies.

Then 500 more.

By the following morning, two other small presses had requested reprint permission. One in Lock Haven, one in Wellsboro.

The story was moving. Not fast. Not loud. But steady.

Just like the river. Just like the roots. Just like whatever had been buried.

And across the valleys and slopes of northern Pennsylvania, the land, and those who lived upon it, stirred as if they remembered something they were never meant to forget.

* * *

The bell above the door chimed five times that morning.

By the sixth, Rebecca Ayers no longer flinched when it rang.

She sat at the corner table in the Cameron County Herald's office, a cup of weak coffee beside her and a growing stack of telegrams and letters unfolding like a second voice alongside her own.

Henry Blodgett, sleeves ink-stained, handed her the latest from the wire clerk. "Came in through Wellsboro. Editor at the *Weekly Courier* wants to reprint Part I. Said he hasn't seen column inches like this in a year, not without someone getting elected or indicted."

Rebecca read the message, lips tight.

Another envelope lay open on the desk beside her. Inside: a handwritten note on a farmer's receipt.

"I remember a girl named Clara. She taught Sunday school one year, in Austin. She said trees could speak if you asked the right way. We all thought she meant poetry. Maybe she didn't."
— L.T., Austin

Another envelope:

"You're not wrong about Fee. He's been buying silence since before I left that ridge. If you need a name to say so publicly, use mine."
— Elijah Harrow, former scale foreman

Rebecca passed the notes to Farnsworth, who stood just inside the doorway with a copy of the latest paper under one arm.

"People are listening," she said.

"They always were," he replied. "They just needed someone brave enough to speak first."

She smiled faintly but didn't let herself relax.

For every message of support, there were others; anonymous scraps, unsigned threats, clipped editorials. One simply read:

You don't understand what you've dug up.

Elmer, seated by the window with his eyes on the alley, didn't look away from the shadows.

"Let 'em threaten," he said. "We've got light now. They've only got matches."

Rebecca nodded and opened the next letter.

This one was from Harrisburg.

Typed. Formal.

Miss Ayers—
We are in receipt of your article and supporting materials. I write to confirm interest in publishing excerpts as part of a public review into timber contracts and suppressed land surveys. You may be contacted for testimony. Please reply by courier.
— A. Blanchard, Office of Forestry Oversight, Harrisburg

Her hands trembled slightly as she set the letter down.

Blodgett looked up from the press.

"You've done it," he said. "You've cracked the bark."

Rebecca didn't reply right away.

She reached into her satchel and pulled out the last page of Clara's journal. The one she had never included in the print.

There's still something beneath the clearing. I don't know what it is. But I know it's not finished. If someone ever reads this… it means it's still listening.

Rebecca stared at the line for a long time.

Then folded the page, sealed it in a blank envelope, and addressed it simply:

To Be Opened Only If I Am Found Missing.

Then she looked at Farnsworth. "We need to go back. Not now. Not loud. But soon."

"Back to the Freck?"

She nodded. "If they're going to bury it again, I want to see what they're burying."

Outside, the wind picked up.

And somewhere, far from town, deeper than roots, older than stories, something turned toward her voice.

Chapter 35 – The Cracks Beneath

October 31, 1898 — Blowville

Terrence Fee hadn't slept in forty-eight hours.

He'd paced the perimeter of the mill yard at dusk, walked the ridge twice before dawn, and now stood alone in the basement of the company office, where the air always smelled of coal dust and rot.

Above him, the tannery hissed and clanked like nothing had changed.

But everything had.

He held the Emporium paper in his left hand, Clara's name bold in ink.

Her words. Her voice. Still alive.

And now believed.

Across the basement, Crane leaned against a support beam, his injured arm in a sling, a fresh welt on his cheek. The riders Fee had sent to intercept Rebecca at Sinnamahoning had not returned.

"I want them found," Fee said quietly.

"They're on the move," Crane answered. "Changing towns every day. Papers are printing faster than we can shut them down."

"Then we stop chasing," Fee muttered. "We start collapsing the ground they're standing on."

He turned toward a shelf stacked with old files, ones not kept in the mill's general ledger. These were the contracts from the early days, before the company had proper stationery. Land trades, timber rights, and... survey reports from 1886.

He opened one with a cracked seal.

Inside, he found the name he was looking for.

Ezekiel Moran – Assistant Scaler / Temporary Constable – Assigned: Freck Warrant

Clara's grandfather.

Fee closed the folder.

He had always known there were roots beneath this thing, but he hadn't known how deep they went. Or how far they reached through blood.

"We silence the past by discrediting the family line," he said. "We'll say Ezekiel was insane. Blame him for the missing surveyors. Say he started the fire of 1887. Clara followed suit."

Crane frowned. "You think people will believe all that?"

Fee looked up, eyes pale and sharp. "No. But they won't be sure. And doubt is enough."

Crane shifted uneasily. "What if the Forestry Bureau opens the warrant?"

Fee set the file down and stepped closer. "Then we give them a reason to stay out. A new danger. Something no one wants to put their name beside."

"Like what?"

Fee looked toward the floor. Toward the earth.

"Disease. Collapse. Madness. Something that kills slow, spreads quiet, and can't be proven."

He stared for a long moment at the stone foundation, where water had begun to leak in from the rain.

Where it looked, he swore, for just a second like the stones were bowing outward, as if something were pushing from the other side.

He blinked.

Gone.

Crane was speaking again, but Fee didn't hear him.

Because in that moment, Fee felt it, not in his ears, but in his chest. A pressure. A hum. Like breath in reverse.

Something beneath Blowville had shifted.

And it was no longer content to wait.

* * *

The lamp flickered once, then went out.

Fee struck a match with shaking fingers and relit it, his breath ragged. He hadn't touched whiskey in three years, but tonight he poured a full glass and drank half before the flame caught.

His hands didn't steady.

He spread the map of the Freck across his desk one more time, marked in old ink and charcoal lines. The clearing was gone now. Burned. Collapsed. But it was still there on the page like a phantom limb.

And next to it, circled faintly, was a symbol he hadn't noticed before.

It hadn't been there last week. It was there now.

A perfect circle. Four intersecting lines. The seal.

He staggered back from the table, knocking over the glass. The map curled under its own weight, as if trying to fold back into silence.

He turned toward the door and called out: “Crane!”

No answer. He called again. Still silence.

Fee stepped out into the hall. The house was dark. Wind rattled the eaves, and somewhere downstairs, the front door creaked; not opening, not closing, just moving.

He gripped the banister.

The floor beneath his boots felt soft. Not wet. Not warped.

Soft. Like bark soaked in rot.

He moved toward the cellar stairs, half-thinking, half-drawn. He didn’t know why. He just knew something had called him down.

The stairs groaned as he descended, lantern in hand.

At the base, the stone wall, old, hand-laid, rough-cut, was sweating.

Not water. Not quite. Something else.

He stepped closer. And there, in the center of the foundation, where mortar had flaked and stone had slumped inward, he saw it:

A gap.

A thin seam, no wider than a knife. It hadn’t been there yesterday.

It pulsed once, like breath.

Fee backed away.

He didn’t remember running up the stairs. He didn’t remember locking the cellar door. But he did remember what Clara had written in her last entry:

If they bury me, it won't be deep enough. And if they bury the truth, it'll dig back out. With claws.

Fee sat down hard in the nearest chair, sweat beading at his collar.

He poured another glass. This time, he spilled most of it.

Outside, the wind had shifted. But the sound wasn't wind anymore. It was movement beneath the house. And Terrence Fee, king of the mill, steward of the timber, master of the silence, realized for the first time…

The land was not his.

It never was.

Chapter 36 – What the Woods Remember

November 1, 1898 — Blowville

It was raining when they found him.

Not a thunderstorm. Not a squall. Just a steady, cold, bone-deep drizzle that made the tannery yard shine like spilled oil. The kind of rain that washes stories clean, or tries to.

The front door to the Fee Brothers mill house stood ajar. No sign of forced entry. No sign of a struggle, not at first. Just a lantern burned low in the hallway and mud where no mud should be, smeared along the stairs, across the walls, even the ceiling.

Crane was the first to step inside. He stopped at the threshold.

"Don't bring anyone else in," he told the yardhand. "Not yet."

The cellar door hung open. And down below, in the hollow beneath the floorboards, something had dug upward.

They found Terrence Fee in his study, slumped in the corner, shirt soaked through, a pistol in his hand that had never been fired.

His face was twisted in something beyond fear. Beyond pain. His eyes were wide, not from violence, but from recognition.

There were no wounds.

No blood.

No sign of what had killed him.

But the room smelled like ash and wet bark, and on the windowpane above his body, something had been scratched into the glass from the inside:

A circle. Four intersecting lines.

Crane stared at it for a long time. He didn't speak. Because there was nothing to say.

* * *

Later, the doctor would list it as "sudden cardiac arrest." The paper in Coudersport would report that Terrence Fee "died peacefully in his home." And the mill would carry on, gears turning, bark steaming.

But in Blowville, people started to speak more softly in the woods.

And at night, when the fog rolled down from the ridges and gathered near the tree line, no one went near the ash ring where the clearing had once been.

They said the ground was hollow there now. That no matter how much dirt you packed in, it always sank by morning.

And some nights, when the moon was high and the wind just right, those who lived close to the Freck said they heard footsteps moving through the underbrush.

Not heavy. Not hurried.

Just steady.

Like someone, or something, was remembering the way back.

Chapter 37 – The Hollow Still Standing

November 12, 1898 — Blowville

They came back just before dusk.

No fanfare. No announcement. Just a wagon pulled quiet through town, wheels creaking over frost-packed ruts, a slow approach down Cameron Road. No one greeted them. No one stopped them. But behind curtains and through cracked doors, people watched.

They saw Sheriff Farnsworth, coat heavy, eyes forward, as he once again passed under the rusted sign that read *Mohan General Store*.

They saw Elmer Fields, older, slower, but still standing, hat in hand as he glanced up at the ruined eaves of the boarding house he'd helped build fifteen years earlier.

And they saw Rebecca Ayers, sitting upright in the back of the wagon, satchel across her lap, eyes on the slope above town, toward where the clearing used to be.

Where the tree once stood.

The ashes were mostly gone now. Wind and rain had done their work. But even from here, she could see the ground still bore the shape of a scar. The slope dipped, unnatural, like something had been peeled away.

They stopped at the Moran house, shuttered since William Moran left it behind. The porch boards sagged, but the bones were good. Elmer tested the door. It opened without resistance.

Inside, the air smelled faintly of dust and pine soap.

Rebecca stepped through slowly.

She was carrying more than papers now. She was carrying the town's memory.

That night, they lit the stove, boiled water for tea, and spread the last of Clara's documents across the kitchen table.

Not for hiding. Not for protection.But for archiving.

Because the story had reached beyond Blowville now. It had made its way to Wellsboro, to Harrisburg, to the halls of state forestry and the ears of editors who had once ignored anything that didn't come printed on timber contracts.

Still, Rebecca knew.

It wasn't finished.

Not the article. Not the fallout. And not the thing beneath the roots.

* * *

They visited Fee's grave the next morning.

It was unmarked.

Buried at the edge of the tannery lot, far from the families he'd once controlled. No sermon. No stone. Just a patch of dirt, flat and quiet.

"He never believed in ghosts," Elmer said.

"No," Farnsworth replied. "But he made one."

Rebecca didn't speak.

She turned toward the slope, toward the Freck, and walked five steps into the trees.

The pines were still. The soil was cold.

But the air no longer felt dead. It felt watchful.

She took the small envelope from her coat, the one labeled *To Be Opened Only If I Am Found Missing,* and tore it in half.

“Not yet,” she said softly.

She turned back toward the town, toward the stove and the papers and the story still forming.

Blowville wasn’t finished. And neither was she.

* * *

Beneath the clearing, where the roots had once wrapped a buried box, the soil had begun to harden again.

No sounds now.

No light.

But the shape remained.

And some things, the land keeps close.

Not to hide.

But to remember.

Part Three

Chapter 38 – Beneath the Stillness

May 23, 1900 — Blowville

The snow had long since melted from the ridges, but the ground beneath the Freck never quite dried.

Mud clung to the roots like memory. Trees leaned a little farther than they should have. And though the clearing had grown over with ferns, it remained colder than the forest around it, as if the earth had not yet forgiven what had been dug out of it.

Blowville had quieted in the year and a half since the fire.

The mill still ran. The tannery still steamed. The whistle still blew at dawn and dusk. But something beneath the routine had shifted. Townsfolk spoke softer near the woods. Hunters no longer camped above the hollow. And the foundation of the old Fee house, though rebuilt in brick, creaked at night with a sound that timber couldn't explain.

They buried Terrence Fee without a marker. No one had argued.

Now his younger brother, Edwin Fee, had returned from Philadelphia to take over the company books. His boots were polished. His collars were stiff. He brought lawyers and ledgers and a new sense of order. But the land didn't care for ink or titles. It remembered the weight of silence, and the things buried under it.

As for Rebecca Ayers, she had not published since *The Hollow Tree*. She remained in Blowville, quiet, watched, and watching. Her late uncle's farm was hers now. So was the Moran house. She tended both.

She wrote often. But she had not sent a single page to print. Not yet.

And that's when he arrived.

Isaac King stepped off the rail line with a rolled jacket, a short stack of carpentry tools, and no idea what had been whispered into the ground he now walked.

He was looking for work.

He would find much more.

Because whatever had stirred beneath the clearing had not gone back to sleep.

It had simply grown patient.

Chapter 39 – The Quiet Watch

May 25, 1900 — Blowville

From the upstairs window of the Moran house, Rebecca Ayers saw him before anyone else did.

He stepped off the midday supply wagon with a tool satchel in one hand and a coat slung over the other. His boots were scuffed but well-kept. He moved like someone who'd built things with care, but not without loss. She recognized the posture. People who came to Blowville rarely did so without leaving something behind.

The man crossed the street slowly, pausing near the post office and glancing at the tannery's main chimney. He didn't look lost, just careful. Newcomers learned quickly here: Blowville didn't offer directions. It waited to see who'd find their own way.

Rebecca watched him from behind the lace curtain, a cup of tea cooling in her hand. She didn't wave. She never did.

After *The Hollow Tree* was published, people treated her like a relic, half-respected, half-feared. No one openly challenged her, but no one confided either. Even now, townsfolk crossed the street a little sooner when they saw her coming. Her house stood quiet at the edge of Main, windows always dark by ten, lanterns lit by six.

She liked it that way.

Most days.

Below, the man, tall, lean, early thirties, approached the mill foreman's office. The door opened. Words exchanged. A handshake.

He'd be staying, then.

Rebecca lowered the curtain and moved back to the writing desk, where a fresh sheet of paper waited, blank except for the words she had written that morning:

The soil hasn't healed. It's only stopped bleeding.

She stared at it for a moment, then set the pen aside.

Down the hall, the floorboards groaned faintly.

She still wasn't sure if it was the wind or the house remembering.

Outside, the whistle sounded for third shift.

And the man named Isaac King took his first steps into the story.

* * *

Isaac King didn't believe in omens.

But he noticed them anyway.

The first was the way the fog never quite lifted from the ridge above the tannery, even though the sun had burned down hard over the rest of the valley. The second was the moss, thick along the foundation stones of nearly every building, as if the town refused to dry out completely.

The third was the way no one had asked him why he came.

Not once.

He'd worked mill towns before. Usually there was small talk. A foreman might ask where a man hailed from, if he'd done beamwork or cut saw tooth. But here? Just a nod, a time to report, and a room key passed from one callused hand to his.

He set his duffel on the bunk in the boarding house. One bed. One chair. A narrow window that looked west toward the creek. The air inside smelled of waxed canvas and boiled coffee. Not unpleasant.

He unpacked slowly.

Laid out his tools. Hammer, awl, square. A worn chisel with "King" etched along the handle in crooked, youthful lines.

It was the only thing his father had left behind when he left.

He didn't dwell on that long.

Instead, he lit the small oil lamp and sat by the window.

From here, he could see the corner of Main Street, the split in the road that led to the old company houses, and beyond them, the line of pine that had been cut too evenly to be natural.

He hadn't asked many questions when he took the job. That had been the point. A town no one talked about unless they were from it, and even then, barely.

He didn't come for answers.

Just quiet.

But even in this first hour, the quiet felt crowded.

Like it was already watching him back.

He caught the briefest movement at the window across the street.

A flick of white curtain. A woman's silhouette.

And then gone.

He didn't know her name yet. But he would.

Chapter 40 – A Good Man With a Quiet Hammer

May 26, 1900 — Blowville

The morning started with sawdust in the boots and coffee boiled too long.

Isaac King stood at the edge of the mill's lumber yard with a set of work orders in his hand and a fresh coat of pine sap already drying on his sleeves. The scent was sharp and clean, but the rest of the place wasn't. The mill was older than it looked, with beams that had been reinforced twice over, and joints so swollen with moisture they creaked like bones in cold wind.

"Most of it's patch work," the foreman had told him. "You keep things from falling in. That's the job."

So he did.

Isaac didn't mind quiet work. He liked the weight of a hammer in his palm, the give of timber under a sharp blade. He liked the way his mind could go still when his hands moved. But even in silence, he listened.

And this town made strange noises.

The mill had its rhythm; gears, pulleys, voices calling loads. But now and then, Isaac heard a pause between the sounds. Like a missing beat. A space where something used to be.

By midday, he had fixed a lintel brace and replaced two rotting steps on the north platform. Sweat clung under his collar. A boy named Orin, no more than sixteen, brought him a pitcher of water and said nothing. Just watched.

Isaac nodded his thanks.

The boy lingered a moment. Then he stated, "You're not from here."

Isaac smiled. "That obvious?"

"Yeah."

"Should I be worried?"

The boy shrugged. "I dunno. Most people leave. You're the first to show up."

Then he walked off.

* * *

Later, while working on a cracked support beam near the back of the lumber shed, Isaac noticed a patch of ground near the edge of the yard where nothing grew. Not even weeds.

The dirt there looked different. Darker. Soft, even though it hadn't rained in a week.

He touched it with his boot. It gave slightly, like there was space beneath it.

He was still staring at the ground when someone cleared their throat behind him.

A tall man with a crooked hat and a limp stood with arms crossed.

"You're new," the man said.

"I am."

"You fixing beams or digging holes?"

"Just noticed the soil was loose."

The man's expression didn't change. "Leave the soil. That ground belongs to the old boundary. Mill doesn't touch it."

Isaac nodded. "Fair enough."

He didn't ask why. He'd already learned the kind of town this was.

When the bell rang for the midday break, Isaac stepped out into the sunlight, which had already begun to fade behind a strange veil of clouds; not storm clouds, but thin and low, like smoke without fire.

He walked the edge of the yard and saw the main road again.

And in the window across the square, a curtain shifted.

She was watching. Again. And he let her.

Chapter 41 – Ledger Ink and Ghosts

May 26, 1900 — Blowville

Edwin Fee preferred a clean desk.

Terrence had not.

His brother's former office had been cluttered with half-filled ledgers, stale tobacco, ink stains, and the scent of sweat that never quite left leather. The windowpanes were caked with smoke. The floorboards were warped where someone had tracked in pitch without wiping his boots.

Edwin had the desk replaced within a week of arrival.

Polished walnut. Brass hardware. Clear lines.

The first thing he did, before hiring a secretary, before adjusting payroll, before even meeting the foreman, was open every ledger Terrence had kept in the final two years of his life.

And they were… revealing.

Scattered notes, strange marks, a few pages torn out. But the margins were what caught his attention.

A name kept appearing, sometimes circled, sometimes underlined.

Crane.

Over and over again.

Fee rubbed his thumb over one of the entries.

—Clearing burned. Crane oversaw delivery. No questions asked.
—If Ayers publishes, Crane will intercept on Pike.
—Cellar marked. Crane confirmed shape intact.

He closed the book.

He remembered Crane, of course, an old woodsman, Terrence's fixer. The man had disappeared shortly after Terrence's death, either gone into the hills or somewhere even quieter.

Edwin tapped the desk lightly with the back of a silver pen.

He was not a man given to superstition. He dealt in property, contracts, tax codes. But the entries unnerved him in their vagueness, their tone.

They read like Terrence had started fearing something he wouldn't name.

And they always came back to Crane.

He called for his assistant.

A quiet, efficient boy named Harold, who knew better than to speak unless prompted.

"Find out if Crane has any known relatives," Edwin said. "If he owns land, owes money, or made enemies. Discreetly."

Harold nodded. "Shall I ask around town?"

"No. Ask in Sinnamahoning. Quiet towns tend to forget faster when the inquiry comes from outside."

Harold paused at the door. "Sir, may I ask…"

"You may not."

The door shut softly behind him.

Edwin stood and walked to the window.

Blowville stretched below, sharp-angled, steam-veiled, and recent by any meaningful measure. It hadn't existed when Edwin was a child; there'd been no reason to visit this part of the county until the trees began to fall and the tannery stacks went up. And yet, looking down at it now, it felt old. Burdened. The kind of place where the soil itself had started keeping secrets. The forest pressed in tighter each year, the treeline creeping toward town like it wanted something back.

He sipped his tea, turned back to the desk, and flipped open a blank journal.

He made a note at the top:

Crane.
No longer on payroll.
Last seen November '98.
Records show increasing irregularities following Terrence's illness.

He underlined "irregularities."

And beneath it, he added:

Journal entries mention Ayers girl.
Investigate further.

He didn't believe in ghosts.

But he believed in unfinished business.

Chapter 42 – Echo Grain

May 29, 1900 — Blowville

By the fourth morning, Isaac King had learned the rhythm of Blowville.

The whistle blew at 6:00. The mill came alive by 6:15. By 6:45, men were either shouting or silent, depending on whether the boilers were cooperating. By 8:00, the smell of steamed bark was thick enough to taste.

He kept his head down. Hammered when asked. Repaired what leaned too far or cracked too loud. Said "yes sir" and "won't be a problem." He took his meals in the boarding house kitchen, where no one asked questions unless they involved the weather.

It was a quiet routine.

But nothing about it felt settled.

The lumber shed still made that slow breathing sound at night, the one that didn't come from wind or tensioned timber. The ground near the back corner of the lot never fully dried. And now and then, he'd find markings in the beams; carvings too deliberate to be accidental, but old enough to be almost erased.

Circles. Lines. One symbol he traced with his thumb and didn't recognize.

He asked Orin, the boy from the yard, if anyone used signs for measurements here. The boy looked at him like he'd spoken in a different language.

"Don't carve in the wood," Orin had muttered. "That's what they told Crane. Before he left."

"Crane?"

Orin went quiet and walked away.

That evening, Isaac skipped dinner and walked east of the tannery, toward the slope that locals avoided without explanation. He told himself he was just clearing his head, that the hills reminded him of work camps in Ligonier or Westmoreland. But the truth sat deeper:

He felt drawn.

The trail wasn't marked, but someone had walked it recently. Moss bent under a single set of boots. A path curved through the underbrush like it had been used more often than anyone admitted.

After half a mile, he reached a clearing that wasn't much of one, just a dip in the earth, overgrown with ferns and brambles, soft underfoot. The trees here leaned away from the center, ever so slightly, like they'd once seen something and decided not to face it again.

Isaac stood there a long time.

Listening.

He didn't hear birds. Didn't hear wind.

Just the sound of his own breath, and something quieter beneath it. Not a voice. Not a sound, even.

Just the weight of memory.

A place that remembered being disturbed.

He turned and headed back before the sun dipped too far, boots heavy, the air colder than it should've been.

At the edge of town, he passed the Moran house again.

And there she was.

Rebecca Ayers.

This time not behind the curtain, but on the porch. Sitting. Watching.

She raised a hand.

Not a wave, just acknowledgment.

He nodded. And kept walking.

But something in the way her eyes followed him said she knew exactly where he'd been.

And what he might be waking up.

* * *

The moment passed quietly.

Rebecca didn't say a word from the porch. Just sat there with her elbows on her knees and a book in her lap, the cover closed. She wasn't reading. She was watching, in that measured, assessing way of someone who'd learned too much about people in too short a time.

Isaac met her eyes. Only for a second.

Then he dipped his head and kept walking, boots crunching gravel in slow, even steps. The air smelled of damp hemlock and burned bark, Blowville's usual mix of rot and labor.

He rounded the next corner, near the footbridge leading toward the rail spur, and nearly collided with a man in a long wool coat and a shoulder-worn revolver holster.

"Steady there," the man said, catching Isaac instinctively by the arm.

Isaac pulled back. "Sorry."

The man squinted at him. Mid-fifties, trim, with a worn face and eyes that didn't miss much. He wasn't dressed like a mill hand, nor like the others who shuffled between the tannery and tavern.

"You're the new one," he said. "Carpenter. King, right?"

Isaac nodded. "That's right."

The man offered his hand. "Farnsworth. Sheriff."

Isaac hesitated, then shook it. The grip was firm, but not showy. A working man's hold.

"Been seeing you walking," Farnsworth added, casual as weather. "Off shift hours. Taking the long way home."

"Just stretching my legs."

"Good place for it," Farnsworth said. Then, after a pause: "Not many walk that trail."

Isaac kept his voice flat. "Didn't see any signs."

"No. That's the trouble."

They stood in a brief silence. Then Farnsworth looked back toward the porch Isaac had just passed. Rebecca was gone now. Door shut. Lamplight in the window.

Farnsworth gave a half-nod. "You spoke to her?"

"No."

"Wise."

Another pause.

"Not that she's dangerous," the sheriff added. "But she's... hard to forget once she starts asking questions."

"I'm not looking for trouble."

"Good," Farnsworth said. "Then I'd recommend staying on this side of the trees. There's work enough in town. And nothing past that ridge ever stays buried."

Isaac met his gaze. "You always greet new workers like this?"

“Only the ones who follow paths that weren’t made for them.”

He gave a courteous nod and walked off toward the station, coat flapping with the wind.

Isaac stood alone in the dark for a long while, watching the lamplight flicker through Rebecca’s window. And wondering just how many people in this town knew more than they were willing to say.

Chapter 43 – Stillness Isn't Silence

May 29, 1900 — Blowville

By the time Rebecca closed the front door, the light had shifted.

That strange, yellowed tint the sky took on when the clouds hung low, but no rain came. The kind of sky Blowville always seemed to wear when something was about to happen.

She stood in the foyer, unmoving.

Behind her, the curtains stirred just slightly though no breeze had come through. The house settled, a low groan in the floorboards, a familiar shift in the stairwell wood. Some people called it age. She'd long since stopped pretending that was all it was.

She had seen him again. The newcomer.

Isaac King.

He hadn't looked afraid when he passed her porch. Just... alert. And he walked like a man who'd learned to read a place before speaking in it.

That made her wary.

Because she'd once walked that same road. And it had cost her everything.

She moved to the parlor and lit the oil lamp, the match crackling in her hand. Shadows pulled back as the light reached the corners of the room, brushing the edge of the shelf where Clara's journal still sat, tucked between county maps and a half-filled ledger of her own.

She hadn't opened it in months. But she never moved it.

It had become something more than memory. A signal. A weight. A promise.

She poured tea that had gone cold and drank it anyway, watching the window. She didn't see him anymore. But someone else had.

Farnsworth.

She'd seen him cross behind Isaac moments after the man passed her porch. The old sheriff never patrolled without a reason, not anymore. And he certainly didn't shadow new hires without cause.

That meant he was already watching.

She wasn't sure if that made her feel better or worse.

* * *

Upstairs, she unlocked the cedar chest at the foot of her bed. Inside lay four bundles, tied letters, unmailed. Not stories. Just observations. Evidence. She added a fifth.

May 29th. New man in town. Isaac King. Walks like a builder, eyes like a reader. Stood at the hollow's edge. Didn't flinch. Watched me. Not in fear. In recognition. What does he recognize?

She tied the page and sealed it with a mark in the corner.

Not Clara's seal. Her own.

She returned the bundle to the chest and stood.

The woods had gone quiet again, but the quiet no longer comforted her. Because she remembered what had happened the last time the town had tried to move on. Something had moved with them.

And it hadn't finished what it came to do.

Chapter 44 – The Threshold

May 30, 1900 — Blowville

Rebecca didn't sleep that night.

Not out of fear, those days were behind her, but because the house had grown too still. And when the house grew still, her mind didn't.

She walked the floor quietly, long past midnight. One circuit around the parlor. Two through the kitchen. Three by the front window, where the lantern by the tannery gates still glowed low and dim.

She hadn't spoken to Isaac King. Not really. Not yet.

But it was already happening again. A stranger had come to town, and something in the ground had noticed.

She could feel it. The old tension, subtle but electric. The way the trees seemed to lean when someone walked too close to the Freck. The way the crows circled low at noon but vanished by dusk. It wasn't just memory.

It was pattern.

And Isaac, knowingly or not, had walked straight into it.

Rebecca returned to her desk and opened the small, worn notebook she kept apart from the rest, not for records, not for writing, but for warnings. Inside, she flipped to the last entry:

Do not speak to those who only see what they want.
Do not walk the trail without a witness.
Do not open the journal again unless the silence begins to shift.

She stared at that last line for a long time.

And then, without ceremony, opened the journal anyway.

The pages still carried the scent of scorched pine. Clara's handwriting, fast, deliberate, moved in clipped loops and careful turns. Rebecca had transcribed parts of it for the article, yes, but much of it had remained unspoken. She'd chosen what to share. She'd chosen what to bury.

But now? Now she wasn't so sure that burying had done anything at all.

She turned to a passage near the end. One she'd memorized but rarely allowed herself to see:

The roots don't stop growing just because we burn the tree. The thing underneath doesn't sleep. It waits. And when it stirs again, it'll come as a question first. A simple one. Like a name.

Rebecca closed the journal.

She stood and walked to the parlor window, as the morning light brought definition to the landscape.

The streets were still empty.

If Isaac was part of this story now, he deserved more than glances across a porch.

He needed truth. And maybe, if she was being honest, so did she.

Chapter 45 – Names That Don't Fade

May 30, 1900 — Blowville

Isaac King knew how to ask questions without making noise.

In towns like Blowville, it wasn't about what you asked, it was how you asked it. Speak too directly and people clammed up. Speak too vaguely and they assumed you were already part of the problem.

So he did what good carpenters always did: he listened first.

Two days after his walk into the woods, Isaac began dropping quiet feelers while loading scrap lumber outside the mill. A half-comment to Orin about how some of the older beams looked rigged up different. A mention to the yardman that someone named Crane had done repairs years back.

Most answers came in shrugs or silence.

"Crane?" one man muttered. "Gone, I think. Or dead. Left when Terrence did."

Another scoffed. "Heard he was touched. Talked to the trees. Bad luck, that one."

But one answer stood out, barely more than a glance.

Old Rudy Barstow, who handled hardware stock and had a tremor in one hand, looked up sharp at the name, then quickly looked away.

"Try the back porch at the cooper's shop," Rudy said. "Midday. You might find someone who remembers more than they'll admit."

So Isaac followed the trail.

The cooper's shop sat just off Main, shuttered most mornings but alive by noon. It was near the old carp shed where the town's benches and wheelbarrows got patched up. Isaac passed it, nodded to the man sweeping out front, and rounded the side.

The back porch was shaded. Quiet. A single chair sat under the eaves, creaking slightly.

And in it sat a man with a beard like silver wire, a cane resting between his knees, and the calm stillness of someone who'd seen the town through both fire and fog.

Elmer Fields.

He looked up before Isaac spoke.

"You're the one asking after Crane," Elmer said. Not a question.

Isaac hesitated. "I am."

Elmer's eyes narrowed, but not unkindly. "You looking to find him?"

"Looking to know who he was. He keeps showing up in places no one wants to talk about."

Elmer tapped his cane once on the porch floor. "He was a man with too many shadows and not enough light. Terrence Fee used him like a prybar, always to break something loose. And when Crane realized what they'd cracked open, it was already too late to put it back."

Isaac stepped closer. "So he ran?"

"No," Elmer said. "He vanished."

"Dead?"

"Maybe. Or maybe he went where no one could follow. He was the last person to step into that hollow after the fire. He said something was still breathing down there. Something not done."

Isaac felt the hairs on the back of his neck rise. "I found one of his marks. Behind the mill."

Elmer's gaze sharpened. "Then you'd better be careful."

"Why?"

"Because marks like that aren't left for the living," Elmer said. "They're warnings. Or invitations. And I don't think Crane ever knew which."

He stood slowly, using his cane.

"You seem like a good man, Isaac. Quiet. But Blowville doesn't stay quiet long. You start digging up names like Crane's, the ground might remember what else is buried with him."

Isaac didn't flinch. "Maybe it's time someone asked anyway."

Elmer gave him a long look.

Then, softer than before: "Then talk to Rebecca Ayers. She's the only one who ever stood close to it and walked away still standing."

And with that, Elmer turned and walked back inside.

Leaving Isaac alone with more than just a name.

Chapter 46 – Between the Lines

June 17, 1900 — Blowville

Three weeks passed.

Isaac King worked his days in sawdust and steam, patched a cracked axle in the tannery cart, rebuilt a beam on the west side of the drying shed. He stopped asking questions aloud, but he didn't stop listening. And Blowville, in its own way, kept whispering.

The ground never fully dried near the edge of the Freck.

Twice, Isaac caught men glancing at him like they'd heard a story that hadn't yet reached him.

Once, someone carved a symbol into the far side of a shed wall. Then scrubbed it clean the next morning.

And through it all, he never saw Rebecca again.

Not until a Thursday afternoon, when the weather broke open and the whole town exhaled under a sharp, cold sun.

Isaac had gone to the general store for nails.

She was already there.

Leaning against the side of the building, coat unbuttoned, arms folded. A satchel hung at her side, but she wasn't shopping.

She was waiting. For him.

They locked eyes before either spoke. Isaac tipped his head. "Miss Ayers."

"Mr. King," she replied. Her voice was calm, but not warm. "Been walking any strange trails lately?"

He gave a faint smile. "Trying to keep to the main roads."

She nodded once. “That’s usually safer. Doesn’t mean it’s right.”

A beat of silence passed between them.

Then he said, “I’ve been looking for someone who could tell me about Crane.”

“I know.”

“You?” he asked.

“No. But the town talks when it thinks you’re not listening.”

Another silence. Then Rebecca straightened. “You’re not from here, Mr. King. That gives you two advantages, and one very big risk.”

“What are the advantages?”

“You don’t owe anyone silence. And you’re not afraid of old names.”

“And the risk?”

“You might think that means the truth is yours to uncover.”

He didn’t answer right away.

Then: “I think something happened here. Something that left marks. In people. In the ground.”

“It did.”

“And you were part of it.”

“I am.”

They stood there for a long moment, not adversaries, not allies, just two people standing at the same page of a different book.

Finally, Rebecca broke the stillness. “I don’t answer

questions in the street," she said. "But if you're not just chasing ghosts, if you actually want to understand, come by the Moran house. Saturday. After supper."

Isaac nodded once. "I will."

Rebecca turned and walked up the road, slow and measured. She didn't look back.

And Isaac, alone now in the dust of the street, felt something shift in his ribs.

Not fear. Not hope. Just the sense that, whatever happened next, the questions were finally going to start getting answers.

* * *

The sun had dipped behind the ridgeline by the time Isaac reached the Moran house.

He stood at the gate for a moment before pushing it open. The path to the porch was narrow but well-kept. No weeds. No scuff marks. The kind of order that came from habit, not vanity.

He knocked once. The door opened before his knuckles fell again.

Rebecca Ayers stood in the frame, one hand resting lightly on the edge. She didn't smile. She didn't look surprised.

"You came," she said simply.

"You asked," Isaac replied.

She nodded once and stepped aside. "Come in."

The interior of the Moran house was warmer than he expected. Faint scent of tea, lamp oil, and something older, cedar, maybe. There were no decorations on the walls. No family portraits. Just books, mostly bound in dark cloth or weathered leather, lined in orderly rows across two low shelves.

She led him into the parlor. The fireplace was unlit, but the oil lamp on the table threw a gentle circle of amber across a stack of papers and a closed journal with a ribbon wrapped around it. Isaac's eyes lingered on it.

She noticed.

"That belonged to Clara Moran," she said. "My friend. The one they tried to erase."

Isaac said nothing.

Rebecca sat in the high-backed chair. She gestured for him to take the one across from her.

"I've read every line," she continued. "Every word she left behind. Some of it I printed. Most of it… I didn't."

"Why not?"

"Because people believe what they're ready to believe. And most of Blowville isn't ready."

Isaac leaned forward slightly. "I might be."

She studied him. "You asked about Crane. He was the last man to stand at the edge of the hollow before everything burned. Before Fee died. Before the clearing caved in."

"People say he vanished."

"They're not wrong. But they're not right, either. Crane saw something. Something they dug up. Something they thought they could bury again."

Isaac's voice lowered. "And you think it's still down there?"

Rebecca didn't answer right away.

Then she opened the ribbon on the journal and turned to the last marked page.

She slid it toward him. In Clara's hand, barely legible beneath a smear of soot:

It isn't buried. It's just patient.

Isaac read the line twice.

Then looked up. "What was under the tree?"

Rebecca looked him straight in the eyes.

"I don't know," she said. "Not exactly. But it was never just about bones. Or secrets. It was about what those secrets fed."

She leaned back in the chair.

"That hollow, what they called the clearing, it's not just a place. It's a wound. And wounds like that don't close without bleeding first."

Isaac let that settle.

The room went quiet. Outside, the wind shifted. A floorboard creaked upstairs, just once.

And for the first time since arriving in Blowville, Isaac King felt something he hadn't yet felt: That he wasn't here by accident.

That the past hadn't just found him. It had called him.

Chapter 47 – Profit and Omission

June 22, 1900 — Blowville

Edwin Fee didn't trust anomalies.

He trusted patterns, margins, projections.

He trusted labor that showed up on time and kept its mouth shut. He trusted the price of bark, the rise and fall of tannin rates, and the fact that most men who came to Blowville wanted one of three things: wages, whiskey, or a way out.

But Isaac King didn't want any of those.

And that made Edwin suspicious.

He'd first noticed the man's name on the May payroll. A carpenter brought in by the foreman, no referrals, no family name attached. Paid on time. Kept to himself. Clean record.

Too clean.

He never visited the saloon or pig's ears. Never gambled. Didn't owe anyone credit at the general store. And yet, he'd spoken with Orin, with Barstow, and now, according to Harold, had been seen speaking with Elmer Fields.

Elmer was a problem in his own right, quiet now, but too observant.

Worse still, Harold reported that Isaac had recently visited the Moran house.

And that was a line Edwin didn't like crossed.

He sat in the office above the mill and turned to the open page of his brother's old ledger.

Crane's name. Again.

Next to a crude diagram of the Freck clearing. No explanation. No coordinates. Just a set of notations:

"They think it's gone."
"But it's not finished."
"Crane says it moves beneath the root line."

Edwin closed the book.

He rose and crossed to the tall cabinet in the corner, unlocked it, and pulled a slim folder from the top shelf. Inside: statements from the coroner, requisition forms for blasting equipment, and an ink sketch of the clearing taken a week after the fire.

He flipped to the bottom. An unsent letter, in his brother's handwriting:

To Crane: if you're still watching the hollow, stay out of the waterline. It's bleeding again.

Edwin didn't know what the line meant. But he knew Crane hadn't been seen since.

And now Isaac was walking the same paths. Asking the same questions. Talking to the same ghosts.

He returned the folder and shut the cabinet.

Then, without hesitation, he rang the bell for Harold. "Find out if King has any family. Back east. West. Doesn't matter. I want a list."

"Yes, sir."

"And speak to Simmons in the tannery. Quietly. Have him follow King for the next week. I want to know when he sleeps, who he speaks to, what routes he walks."

Harold nodded and left.

Edwin turned back to the window, staring down at the town. At the slope behind it. At the trees that never seemed to grow closer or farther, just always there.

Terrence had died chasing something in those woods.

But Edwin didn't believe in ghosts.

Only in liabilities. And Isaac King had just become one.

Chapter 48 – When the Reins Are Cut

July 3, 1900 — Blowville

It happened fast.

A sudden shout, the crack of hooves on stone, and the sound of a wagon wheel splitting in two.

By the time Isaac reached the edge of the tannery yard, dust was still settling. A black gelding, wide-eyed and heaving, stood tangled in broken tack near the supply shed. Two barrels had burst on impact, soaking the mud with dye. A wheel rim spun loose in the grass.

And in the center of it all lay Sheriff Farnsworth; motionless, one leg twisted beneath him, his coat torn across the back.

Men rushed in, but Isaac was already there, dropping to one knee beside him. "Easy, Sheriff. Stay still."

Farnsworth's breath was shallow. One side of his face was scraped and bleeding.

He blinked up at Isaac with a flicker of recognition, and then something else.

Regret.

* * *

By evening, word had spread.

The doctor from Austin was sent for, though there was little he could do. A cracked hip, a broken wrist, and a spine too old to risk more time in the valley.

Farnsworth was moved to the old station house for the night, but by morning, arrangements were made.

He would leave for Ebensburg by rail. His sister had room. And patience. And far fewer hills.

Rebecca stood at the platform when the train pulled out. She didn't wave. Farnsworth didn't look back.

And just like that, Blowville was without a sheriff.

* * *

Two days later, Isaac stood outside the general store, arms folded, watching a group of boys dare one another to throw rocks at the old company bell.

They weren't malicious, just unchallenged. But it stirred something in him.

That night, he walked the length of the town twice. Down past the tannery, up toward the ridge, then back through the main street.

The quiet felt different now. Less held. Less watched.

In the morning, he asked a few questions. Just simple ones.

How did the county appoint a replacement? Who managed law when the seat was empty?

No one gave a straight answer.

Some said the mill foreman would "keep order." Others mumbled that the Fee Brothers would "make arrangements." But most just looked away and said:

"We'll manage."

But Isaac could already feel the drift.

He found himself back in front of the Moran house that evening.

He didn't knock. Just stood outside, staring up at the lamplight in the second window.

Then he walked home and sat at the desk in his rented room.

He stared at the sheriff's star someone had quietly left on his bunk. He didn't pick it up. But he didn't put it away either.

Because something told him Blowville wasn't going to stay quiet for much longer.

And when things turned, someone needed to be standing at the edge.

* * *

It was past ten when Isaac returned to the Moran house, this time not just standing at the gate.

He knocked once.

A lantern was lit on almost instantly. She'd been awake.

Rebecca Ayers answered the door, her shawl already wrapped around her shoulders. "I figured it was you."

Isaac looked tired. But something in his posture had changed, like a man who'd stopped asking if he was ready and had begun accepting that no one ever is.

"Can I ask you something?" he said.

She nodded and stepped aside.

He didn't sit. Just hovered near the coat rack, holding the sheriff's star in one hand like it had a weight it hadn't earned yet.

"I never came here to stay," he began. "Didn't come to fix a town or settle debts that aren't mine. But something's shifting. And I can feel it starting to lean the wrong way again."

Rebecca crossed her arms. "It never stopped. It just paused. Long enough for the next wave to forget what the last one cost."

He nodded. "That's what I'm afraid of."

She studied him for a moment. "You think a badge makes a difference?"

"No," Isaac said. "I think standing still while no one else will does."

That brought the faintest twitch of a smile from her. Not approval. Just understanding.

"Farnsworth kept order," she said, "because people knew what he wouldn't tolerate. You won't scare them like he did."

"I'm not trying to."

"Then what are you trying to do?"

He looked at the star again. "I want to be a name they don't whisper when something goes wrong. I want them to say it out loud, and know it means someone will show up."

Rebecca was quiet for a long moment.

Then she said, "Then wear it. And remember that what's buried here isn't done shifting. Law alone won't hold it."

Isaac nodded, and this time, he clipped the badge onto the inside of his coat, not for show, but for readiness.

As he turned to leave, Rebecca added, "You'll need help."

He paused. "You offering?"

"I'm offering a warning," she said. "The next thing to rise out of that ground won't wait for permission."

He nodded once, solemnly. "I won't either."

And with that, he stepped back into the night.

A carpenter. A watcher. A reluctant sheriff. And the last man in Blowville willing to stand between the roots and the rest of them.

Chapter 49 – The Stranger with the Star

July 6, 1900 — Blowville

The badge wasn't announced.

It simply appeared.

Pinned low on Isaac King's inner coat, just visible when he moved through the square or stood at the edge of a work crew. He didn't carry a revolver, didn't patrol on horseback, didn't raise his voice.

But people noticed.

They always noticed.

At the mill, men started nodding to him differently, not with respect, exactly, but with pause. The way one might nod to a storm cloud and hope it passes by.

At the tannery, Simmons muttered, "A carpenter in a sheriff's coat," to no one in particular. But the next day, the tannery bell rang on time and no one went home drunk.

At the general store, Mrs. Mohan asked Isaac if he was there to collect a tax. When he shook his head, she squinted and said, "Then wear that thing proud, or not at all. People don't trust a badge that hides."

Isaac nodded, but didn't adjust it. The badge stayed where it was, close to the chest.

* * *

The younger ones, though, Orin and his kind, watched him differently.

They followed at a distance.

They saw how he spoke to the elders, how he listened more than he answered. They saw how he walked alone in the evenings and checked the corners of the rail yard where others avoided.

They saw, too, how he passed the old Fee house and never turned his head.

He wasn't afraid of it. He wasn't afraid of much, it seemed.

But there was one morning, four days after he first wore the star, when he stood too long at the edge of the clearing.

Just staring into the woods, unmoving.

Orin watched from the slope above.

He saw Isaac's hand brush against the badge.

Not protectively. But like a reminder.

As if to say, *I chose this. I'm still choosing.*

And maybe that was enough.

* * *

At the edge of town, Elmer Fields smoked on his porch and nodded as Isaac passed.

"Took guts," he muttered.

Behind him, his wife said, "We'll see if it was guts or foolishness."

* * *

At the Moran house, Rebecca wrote the town's name at the top of a fresh page in her journal.

Blowville. Still held together by timber, tannin, and the thinnest thread of will.
And now, a stranger wears the star. Not to control it. But to hold the line.
Just like Clara tried. Just like Elmer stood. Just like

Farnsworth endured.
Maybe, finally, the line will hold.

She closed the book.

And somewhere beneath the ground, the hollow waited.

Watching. Listening. Measuring what kind of sheriff this stranger would become.

* * *

Edwin Fee didn't read gossip.

He read ledgers.

Production rates, transport delays, timber rights. He studied the cost of lime and leather and the quiet erosion of worker loyalty. He made decisions based on numbers, not whispers.

But that morning, Harold brought a name instead of a number. "King's wearing the badge."

Edwin didn't look up from his desk. "What badge?"

"Farnsworth's. Town's calling him sheriff now."

There was a long silence. Outside, the mill whistle screamed the midday shift change.

Edwin closed the ledger with slow precision. "Does he have an appointment from the county?"

"No. But no one's contested it. Not yet."

"And Ayers?"

"Hasn't said a word publicly. But she's seen walking with him. Twice."

Edwin stood and moved to the window, hands clasped behind his back. From here, he could see the entire curve of

Main Street; the rooftops, the dirt track, the low sag of the Moran porch.

“Who gave him the badge?” Edwin asked.

“No one knows.”

“Then someone wanted it that way.”

He tapped the glass once. “I want you to speak with Simmons again. No more watching. Start nudging. Quietly. We remind the town that order doesn’t come from sentiment.”

Harold shifted. “He’s not exactly sentimental.”

“Then remind them that order has a price.”

Harold paused. “And if he pushes back?”

Edwin turned sharply. “Then we remind him what happened to the last man who stood in front of a secret he didn’t understand.”

A pause.

Then softer, almost to himself: “They always think it’s about justice. Until they find the roots.”

* * *

That night, Edwin sat in his office long after the lamps burned low.

He reopened Terrence’s old folder.

The unsent letters. The notes about Crane. The drawing of the clearing.

And a final phrase, written in a narrow line across the bottom margin of the last page:

When the law grows teeth, the woods stop whispering.

Edwin didn't know whether it was meant as a warning, or a wish. But either way, he knew Blowville had changed again. And for the first time since returning, he no longer felt alone in the dark.

Chapter 50 – The Pattern Beneath

July 8, 1900 — Moran House

Rebecca Ayers had stopped keeping a daily journal when the ground first froze that winter.

She told herself it was because nothing had changed. The fire was out. The silence had returned. And for a while, the town had honored its uneasy truce with memory.

But now?

Now, she was writing again.

She sat at the desk in the parlor, pen steady, ink dark.

It's beginning again. Not in fire. Not in fear. In movement. Quiet ones. Men leaning in when they think no one sees. Edwin in his window. Harold walking loops that aren't casual. Simmons speaking in corners.

And Isaac, steady, listening, holding ground like someone who doesn't know whether to stay or run. But still standing.

She paused, listening to the wind brush the shutters.

The trees had changed. They leaned in again. Subtle. Like they were drawing closer with each breath.

She knew the signs.

It was how it started before. Not with screams. But with shadows. And footsteps in the fog.

She rose and crossed to the window. The street was empty, save for a cat moving between stoops.

Then, in the lamplight across the square, she saw Harold.

Edwin's clerk. Standing still. Watching.

He moved on after a moment. But not fast. Not afraid. Just cataloguing. Quiet surveillance.

Rebecca drew the curtain closed.

She no longer feared Edwin Fee. But she respected his instinct for pressure. And right now, he was looking for cracks.

She walked upstairs and opened the cedar chest.

Inside: her notes, Clara's journal, the copies of the original story, hidden and bound.

She didn't touch them.

Instead, she retrieved a small folded letter, one she'd never mailed. It was addressed to a man in Harrisburg. Forestry Bureau. Someone who'd believed her once.

If something shifted again, she would send it.

And not for publication. But for excavation. Because if the signs were true, and they usually were, the roots beneath the hollow were moving again.

And this time, they weren't going to stay buried.

* * *

There was a knock at the door just after eleven.

Not urgent. Not careless. Measured.

Rebecca already knew who it was before she opened it.

Isaac stood on the porch, hat in hand, coat damp at the shoulders from the rising mist. He looked tired in a way she understood; not from labor, but from watching everything too closely for too long.

"I shouldn't have come this late," he said.

"But you did," she replied.

She stepped aside.

He entered without needing directions, without hesitation. That was something she noticed about him: he never looked lost in her house.

She poured two cups of tea without asking. Neither of them spoke for a full minute.

Then Isaac said, "Edwin's watching you."

She nodded. "I know."

"He's watching me too."

Another nod.

Isaac looked at the bookshelf. The same worn leather spines. The journal still on the desk, wrapped now in a cloth band.

"Do you ever regret it?" he asked.

"Publishing?" Rebecca said. "No."

"Staying."

She didn't answer right away.

Then: "Sometimes I think I stay because no one else would know where to look if something rose again."

He looked at her. "You still think it might?"

She looked back. "Don't you?"

A silence stretched out between them. Not awkward, just dense.

Isaac set down his cup. "I found something behind the mill today. A stone outcropping near the rear shed. Looked natural at first, but it wasn't. Someone shaped it. Chiseled a groove down the center. Maybe years ago."

Rebecca's voice was low. "Crane left marks like that. Paths. Signals. Things only a few could read."

"I think someone's trying to erase them now."

"That means they're afraid."

Another silence.

But it shifted. Warmer now. Not soft, exactly, but familiar. Like two people who had stopped testing each other and started seeing.

She stood to refill her cup, brushing close past him as she moved. He didn't step back.

She felt the pause in him, like a word half-spoken.

When she turned, she caught him looking at her. He didn't look away. She didn't either.

Nothing was said. Nothing needed to be.

But in that moment, the room felt different.

No longer just a space for strategy or secrets.

It felt… shared.

Isaac broke the silence first. "If this stirs again, I won't run."

"I know," she said.

And for the first time, she smiled. Not out of relief.

But out of recognition.

Chapter 51 – Marks That Weren't Meant to Last

July 9, 1900 — Behind the Mill

The mist hadn't lifted by dawn.

Isaac left the boarding house before the tannery whistle blew, boots crunching on gravel, breath forming quiet clouds in the half-light. The streets were empty. Lamps flickered out. Somewhere down the slope, a dog barked once and fell silent.

He didn't head toward the yard.

He went to the back of the property.

Beyond the tool sheds and behind the drying racks, there was a slope where old machinery was dumped; broken gears, rusted coils, warped siding. No one went back there unless they had a reason.

Isaac had one now.

The stone sat where he'd remembered. Just beyond the second lean-to, near a patch of bramble that never quite took root.

He crouched beside it.

It looked natural, at first. A slab of sandstone, pitted and dull. But someone had shaped its center. A long, narrow groove ran straight through the middle, not deep but deliberate. And along the edge, just faintly, a carving:

A circle. Split four ways by lines.

The same symbol Clara had drawn. The one Rebecca had shown him.

He ran his thumb over it.

Someone had tried to chisel it out, scarring the edge, hacking shallow crosses through it. But the shape remained.

It was old. But not forgotten.

Isaac looked around. The air felt heavier back here, not damp, but dense, like the woods were holding their breath.

He walked the perimeter, searching for more.

And found a second stone, half-buried. This one had no symbol. Just a pair of notches, one vertical, one diagonal, aligned like a compass.

He squinted and followed the direction they pointed.

Toward the northern slope, just beyond the clearing's former edge.

A path long overgrown, but still walkable.

And beside it, in the weeds: an old boot print.

Fresh. Not his.

He didn't follow it.

Instead, he returned to the first stone and pulled a stub of chalk from his coat pocket. He traced the shape carefully, line by line, onto a slip of folded paper.

Then he stood and listened.

The tannery whistle broke the silence, shrill and mechanical.

But beneath it… he thought he heard movement.

Something soft. Not animal. Not water.

The sound of weight shifting underground.

* * *

Later that day, Isaac would slip the chalk drawing across Rebecca's kitchen table.

She would stare at it. She would not speak.

But her hand would rest, for a long moment, on the spine of Clara's journal.

And they would both know: the ground wasn't done speaking. It was just beginning again.

Chapter 52 – The Overgrown Path

July 10, 1900 — North of the Freck

Rebecca didn't need a compass.

She had the drawing. The notches. And Isaac's quiet confidence in the way he'd traced the groove on the stone. He hadn't said it aloud, but she saw it in his posture: he felt something under that ground. And now, so did she.

She moved carefully.

The path wasn't much more than suggestion: damp ferns, flattened thorns, and the occasional indent of old boot prints. But it followed a consistent slope, curving through pine and maple stands that had long outgrown their cut lines.

Birdsong faded the farther she walked.

Even the wind seemed reluctant here.

Just before the ridge opened up, she found the second stone.

Lower than Isaac had described. Almost buried in loam and moss. But she could see the same notches. The same deliberate angle.

She knelt beside it and ran her fingers along the edge. Beneath her palm, the stone felt warm.

That wasn't right. The sun hadn't reached this part of the woods yet. She stood again and kept walking.

The slope leveled out. The canopy broke. And suddenly, she was standing at the edge of a low depression in the earth, no more than thirty feet wide, ringed with wild grass and saplings.

But she knew this place.

It had once been the hollow tree's root bed.

The tree was gone now. Burned. Collapsed. Nothing but black soil and the faint memory of shape.

But the center…

The center still looked wrong.

She approached carefully. Her boots sank slightly in the loose ground. She stepped around the outer rim, where fungus bloomed in too-perfect circles and ferns grew in spirals rather than clusters.

And then she saw it.

Cloth.

Half-rotted. Nestled in the dirt. Just a few inches showing, a ragged sleeve.

She crouched and brushed away a layer of soil. Her hand froze.

Bone.

Wrist. Forearm. Discolored. Long buried, but not yet reclaimed.

And below it, collapsed in the center of the hollow…

A ribcage. Torn. Sunken.

And a shoulder socket separated from its limb.

The left hand was gone.

Rebecca stepped back quickly, heart pounding, breath short. But not from fear. From certainty.

“Crane,” she whispered.

There was no way to know for sure. No face. No tools.

But in her gut, in the marrow of memory and all the pieces Clara never got to finish, she knew.

Crane had come here last.

And he had never left.

* * *

She stayed a few more minutes, marking the area with small stones and branches in case the rain came.

Then she turned and made her way back down the path.

By the time she reached the Moran house, the sun had begun to climb. Isaac was already waiting on the porch.

He stood when she approached, and she didn't say a word.

She just nodded once, slowly. And he understood.

They would go back together.

But now, they were no longer searching for what had happened. They were preparing for what it still meant. And neither one of them was planning to face it alone.

Chapter 53 – Morning Knows

July 11, 1900 — Moran House

Morning came slowly to Blowville.

The kind of soft, overcast light that filtered through the trees like breath. No wind. No sound of distant hammers or tannery steam. Just the steady, unhurried silence of a town waiting.

Rebecca stood at the kitchen window, hands wrapped around a cup of tea she hadn't touched.

The hollow was still with her. The bones. The missing hand. The shape of something that hadn't died right.

She didn't need to ask Isaac if he understood. He had.

Last night, when she returned from the woods, mud-streaked, silent, he didn't press her. He just waited. Sat by the fire and listened as she told him what she'd seen. No questions. Just clarity.

Now, she could feel him moving in the room behind her. Quiet footfalls. The creak of floorboards adjusted to a second presence.

She didn't turn until she heard the water boil.

He'd made coffee. Without asking.

She watched as he poured a cup and placed it beside her, then leaned against the opposite wall with his own.

"You sleep?" he asked.

"A little," she said. "You?"

"Enough."

Neither spoke for a long moment.

Then she said, “It’s him. I don’t know how, but I know.”

“Crane.”

She nodded.

Isaac exhaled through his nose. “What now?”

“We go back,” she said. “Together.”

He watched her a moment longer. Then: “You always talk like it’s you against the woods.”

She met his gaze. “It has been.”

“It’s not anymore.”

That stopped her. She didn’t speak for a beat.

Then she turned fully to him. “It’s dangerous.”

“I know.”

“You could leave.”

“I won’t.”

A quiet settled again.

But it wasn’t tense. It wasn’t waiting for something to break.

It was trust.

The kind that had grown between them slowly, like roots beneath frostline. Unspoken, but strong.

Rebecca reached for her shawl. Isaac moved toward the door. And without needing to say anything more, they stepped outside together, toward the trail, toward the hollow, and toward whatever remained beneath it.

* * *

The path was quieter than yesterday.

Not because it was empty, but because it recognized them now.

The forest didn't resist their presence. It simply watched.

Rebecca led without speaking, steps sure-footed, hand brushing saplings as she passed. Isaac followed close, boots careful on the moss-soft ground. They brought no tools. Just lanterns. Just presence.

The silence between them wasn't empty.

It held reminders.

* * *

She had never met Clara Moran.

But she'd read her words so many times that they felt etched into her ribs. Ink-dark confessions, written by a woman who saw too much and survived too little. Rebecca hadn't been handed the journal. She'd inherited it, pages passed down like a final breath no one was brave enough to exhale.

She hadn't forgotten.

But remembering hadn't saved anyone.

Now she walked not in Clara's shadow, but in her place, to finish what had been left undone.

* * *

He remembered a different silence.

A morning in McKeesport, the sound of hammer against splintered beam, and his father walking out the door for the last time. No goodbye. No letter.

Just a vanished shadow, and the sharp lesson: some men

run because they're afraid of what staying might make them face.

Isaac had run too, until he came here.

Now?

Now he walked beside a woman who had never run, even when the ground opened beneath her.

And that steadied him.

* * *

They reached the first stone.

Rebecca paused to touch the groove again. This time, she didn't flinch.

"The trees weren't like this before," she said. "They're growing inward now."

Isaac looked up. She was right. The branches overhead reached toward the hollow, like they were bracing it, or pointing at it. Not natural. Not wild.

Intentional.

"We're close," he said.

They stepped into the clearing.

The depression hadn't changed overnight. The broken soil still bore its uneven breath. The remains, half-buried, half-exposed, rested just as she'd left them.

Rebecca crouched beside the ribs. Isaac knelt near the edge. Neither touched the bones.

They simply stood witness. And that, more than anything, seemed to change the air.

A breeze passed through the hollow. Soft. Then still. And

Rebecca, without knowing why, reached over and took Isaac's hand.

He didn't speak.

He just held it.

Because the past could take everything, names, silence, even skin and bone, but what stood here now was new.

And it wasn't afraid.

Chapter 54 – What the Ground Keeps

Two Days Later — The Hollow

The clearing was quiet again.

No wind. No birdsong. Just the hush of trees leaning inward, not like mourners this time, but like witnesses.

Isaac King stood at the edge of the hollow, spade in hand, his boots sunk into soft ground. He hadn't moved in several minutes.

The bones were wrapped. The hole was ready. But still, he hesitated.

Behind him, Rebecca Ayers crouched beside the bundle. It was smaller than it should have been. A ribcage. Part of a jaw. The right hand, curled inward like it still remembered holding something it shouldn't.

The left hand was missing.

They hadn't spoken on the walk up. There wasn't much to say. Because this wasn't a man they mourned.

Crane had been a servant of silence, a hand that enforced the will of the Fee family. He'd hurt people. Covered things. Made others disappear.

And still… he had come here, alone.

And died in the dirt.

"I don't think he deserves a grave," Isaac said, finally.

Rebecca didn't argue.

But she said, "Then maybe we're not giving him one."

Isaac looked over.

“We're not burying him to honor him,” she said. “We're burying what's left. What's trying to cling to the surface. We do it for the town. For the land.”

He nodded once, jaw tight. And then he dug.

The earth gave easily, too easily, like it wanted Crane gone as much as they did.

When the hole was ready, Rebecca stepped forward with the bundle. She didn't speak. She didn't linger.

She laid him down like someone closing the last page of a book that never should have been written.

Together, they filled it back in. No marker. No stone.

Just a sapling, taken from the ridge's edge, planted with slow, deliberate hands. A living thing where a violent man had fallen.

Not a grave. A warning. A beginning.

* * *

They sat at the edge of the clearing afterward, both covered in soil, boots streaked with rot. The tree stood behind them, small and slight.

But already rooted.

The silence was different now.

Not forgiving. But watchful.

Isaac was the first to speak. “You think something like that… like him… just ends?”

Rebecca shook her head. “No. But something else starts when we put it in the ground.”

He looked at her. “Are we safer now?”

“I don’t know,” she said. “But we’re not afraid.”

That seemed to settle something between them.

He reached for her hand. She let him.

Not as comfort. As recognition. Because this wasn’t peace. But it was a choice. And sometimes, that had to be enough.

Chapter 55 – Settling the Dust

July 21, 1900 — Moran House

The summer settled in soft that year.

The tannery ran quieter. The mill's rhythm grew steadier. And Blowville, as if it had spent itself on grief and suspicion, finally began to sleep through the night again.

No more signs carved into stone.

No more whispers in the woods.

Just the ordinary creak of floorboards and the scent of cut timber rising with the morning steam.

At the Moran house, Rebecca kept the windows open longer now. The journals were still on the shelf, but they gathered less dust. Isaac had patched the loose stair plank and replaced the hinges on the kitchen door. He didn't say much about staying.

He just stayed.

Their lives had taken on a rhythm of small, deliberate things.

He made the coffee before sunrise.

She walked the edge of the property at dusk, listening to the wind in the pines.

They didn't talk about what was under the tree anymore.

They didn't have to.

* * *

Once, a man from Coudersport came asking questions, said he was with the land office, wanted to confirm mineral rights near the Freck. Rebecca sent him away with a map that had no mention of the clearing.

When Isaac asked why, she said, “Because some places need to be remembered. Others need to be left alone.”

He didn’t argue

* * *

They never marked Crane’s grave.

But the sapling they planted grew fast, too fast for the soil, too fast for the season.

It wasn’t unnatural. But it wasn’t ordinary, either.

Rebecca tended it when she could.

Isaac kept watch from the edge of the treeline, hat in hand.

The town didn’t ask what they were doing. And maybe, finally, it didn’t need to.

Chapter 56 – All Hallows' Eve

October 31, 1900 — Blowville

By October, the sapling had grown over four feet tall.

Its leaves were late to turn, still green when every other maple and ash had gone gold and red. Its trunk was thicker than it should have been, its roots too deep for five months' growth. The townspeople whispered about it. No one went near.

But Rebecca Ayers trimmed the grass around it every other week.

And Isaac King, sheriff still, though he never wore the badge in town, walked a slow circle around it when he passed.

They didn't speak of the tree. Not in words.

But they both watched it. And they both knew.

* * *

That night, All Hallows' Eve, the wind shifted strangely.

It wasn't a storm wind. It didn't howl or snap. It crept.

It moved through the eaves of every house in Blowville, tapped gently on shutters, stirred ash in the hearths, and paused, just briefly, outside the homes of those who had forgotten what had come before.

And in the Fee Brothers' house, where no fire had been lit in two nights and the doors were always locked too tightly, something came knocking.

Edwin Fee sat at his desk, a decanter of rye half-full and untouched. He'd been writing letters. Long ones. Not to be mailed.

When the knock came, he didn't move.

It was a single tap.

Then another. Then silence.

When he finally opened the door, nothing stood on the stoop.

But the wind rushed past him into the house, curling through the room like smoke, heavy with the smell of pine and old earth.

And for the first time since Terrence's death, Edwin felt afraid.

Not of what had come. But of what had agreed to leave.

He never spoke of it. Not even to Harold. But the next morning, he canceled two land claims near the Freck. Quietly. Without explanation.

And the tree kept growing.

* * *

Later that week, Rebecca and Isaac sat on the porch of the Moran house, a quilt across their laps, a pot of tea cooling on the step.

He reached for her hand without looking.

She didn't pull away.

No vows. No rings. But Blowville knew.

They were married before the first frost. And they never left.

Not because they feared the thing beneath the roots, but because they understood it.

Some places don't heal. Some things stay buried because they are watched. And as long as someone keeps watch…

The peace holds.

Even if it isn't perfect.

Even if the wind still shifts strangely now and then.

Especially on nights like this.

Epilogue

Present Day — King's Camp, Potter County

The campfire had burned low, down to coals that pulsed red beneath a lattice of split pine.

Marin Clarke leaned forward, elbows on her knees, letting the heat soak into her palms. Beyond the light, the trees stood tall and black, their silhouettes older than the country itself. She could still smell the tang of the First Fork in the air, a whisper of tannin and rain-soaked stone.

Across from her, Jim King poured the last splash of bourbon into his tin cup.

"That's the story," he said.

Marin looked at him, the firelight casting soft gold in the lines around his eyes. He was nearly seventy now, with a voice that carried quiet authority and the patience of someone who'd spent most of his life listening to the land.

She let the silence stretch.

Then: "You really believe all of it?"

Jim shrugged. "Doesn't matter if I believe it. Isaac did. Rebecca did. And they stayed. Married. Never had children of their own, but they raised this place like it was one."

He pointed past the fire, toward the shadowed outline of the house beyond the trees.

"You've already been inside," Jim said. "The Moran house."

Marin nodded. "The journal pages. Clara's hand."

Jim took a slow sip from his tin cup. "That house has stood since the 1880s. Isaac never left it. Rebecca either. Folks say they kept the windows facing the woods clean, like they were always watching."

He shifted, staring into the fire.

"My family's had this camp for generations, but none of us ever lived here full-time. Hunting, fishing, summers mostly. But we always looked out for the house. Fixed a shutter here, cleared a path there. Quiet work. Like tending a grave."

Marin glanced toward the darkened porch, remembering the creak of the floorboards, the way the dust lay thick but undisturbed, the weight of history pressed into the walls.

"It still feels... watched," she said.

Jim didn't disagree.

"Some houses forget," he murmured. "That one remembers."

She looked out into the trees. The wind had picked up, rattling a loose shutter on the storage shed. Somewhere far off, an owl called.

"So, the tree?" she asked.

Jim followed her gaze toward the edge of the clearing.

"Lightning took it down in the '40s. But it burned for three days. In the rain."

Marin said nothing.

He took a long sip. "My grandfather swore he saw something standing where the roots were, just before the last flame went out. Never described it. Just said it didn't look surprised."

Marin leaned back against the log and looked up at the stars.

"So why tell me now?"

Jim King smiled again, this time gentler.

"Because the woods are quieter when someone's watching. You wanted to write about this place. Just figured you should know what it's already written."

She sat with that a while.

Then she asked, "Do you think the peace held?"

He looked at the fire, then at the woods.

"I think it still is."

And for a while, neither of them spoke.

The fire hissed softly.

The forest, just beyond the ring of light, waited.

But it did not come closer.

Not tonight.

www.ingramcontent.com/pod-product-compliance
Lightning Source LLC
LaVergne TN
LVHW091127080826
845145LV00008B/2069
* 9 7 8 0 9 9 6 4 3 9 6 6 4 *